IGNITED!

or

zz's

by
Will Bernard

ig·nited!
ig·nit·ed, ig·nit·ing

: to subject to fire or intense heat;
especially : to render luminous by heat

: to set afire

: to heat up : excite

: to set in motion : spark

jolt
verb

: to cause (something or someone) to move
in a quick and sudden way

: to move with a quick and sudden motion

: to surprise or shock (someone)

IGNITED!
or
zz's Jolt

by
Will Bernard

Lenzvision Publishing

Edited by Pam Thomas
Book Design by Patty Atcheson-Melton

All rights reserved, including the right of reproduction
in whole or in part in any form.

ISBN:978-0-692-01857-6

I promised to dedicate this book to Dad and Mom,
and they promised to never read it.

Special thanks to Midori
Inspired by Penny L'Amour
Blessing on muses and nymphs!

Contents

Buzzin'

11

What About the Women?

16

Leaving Limbo

26

Naneeka

29

May I Feel, Said He

33

Come On Up

44

Sweet Puberty

48

Me Tarzan, You Jane?

53

Me Jane, Where's Tarzan?

56

Lucy Dares DJ to Dance the D/s

59

Seeking An Oasis
70
❧

Honeywater
76
❧

Volcanic Eruptions
82
❧

Red
89
❧

Piper's Diary
93
❧

Pipertoy
100
❧

zz Gets ZZ'd
110
❧

Birthday Suited
112
❧

Forked Road
118
❧

About the Author
121
❧

"You will hardly know who I am or what I mean,
But I shall be good health to you nevertheless,
And filter and fibre your blood.

Failing to fetch me at first, keep encouraged.
Missing me one place, search another;
I stop somewhere, waiting for you."

-"Song of Myself", Walt Whitman

Buzzin'

i lost my home,

lone bee, no hive.

may not have much

but still i thrive

buzzin', lovin',

breathin', alive!

feelin' spicy!

little older, gettin' gray.

i still got game;

i'm comin' your way!

- zz's journal

When his 25-year marriage fell apart, the entire tapestry unraveled, strands sailing off in the wind like kite tails freed from the kite. Zachary Zeebo Jolt (modified from O'Joltern upon his great-great-grandparents' immigration), had crashed and burned. He had spent just over a year shut away in the bedroom of the house he and his wife had shared, drinking Rumpunch! and smoking three cherry pipe tobacco. Jobless, connections to friends and family broken or in disrepair, bankrupt, and a month away from eviction, zz was drowning and didn't much care. Dr. Gravel Rasp, Professor Emeritus, Lenzonian Physics, sent in the lifeline.

zz had ignored any pounding on the front door for months, and today was no exception. It stopped after a bit. But Dr. Rasp was not about to give up! He walked around back, and was not surprised to find the sliding glass door to the den unlocked. He entered and moved silently to zz's bedroom door, then knocked and opened the door.

zz was smearing some pastels on canvas when the knock came, and his head popped up, irritation quickly turning to delight. It was Gravel Rasp, his friend of over 40 years! Dr. Rasp was a very, very busy man; they were rarely able to meet in person. zz offered a chair and a glass; they smiled widely in unison: Rumpunch! Clink of the glasses, and Gravel said, "To a bountiful future!"

Taking their seats, they sipped and talked of this and that, mostly sports. They downed another glass quickly, and as the glow set in Dr. Rasp, in his gracious manner, asked if zz was interested in a business venture.

Gaunt, jobless...soon homeless...zz laughed out loud! "Me, an asset?"

Holding out his glass for a refill, Gravel said, "I have a need to invest some funds in a business venture that will fail. I need a steady, dependable source of lost revenue." They smiled, eyeball to eyeball. zz grabbed the pitcher of Rumpunch! and refilled the glasses.

"You want me to lose your money?"

"I need some tax adjustments," Gravel said. "If I can accurately predict a yearly loss of revenue on a non-profit business, that will shift my tax base, and enable some expansion in other areas. It's a situation you could handle better than most anyone

I know. I need a disc jockey. You will receive a monthly salary, and the rest of the investment will be in rent, promotions, and advertising. You are about to become the one and only disc jockey on the world's smallest radio station."

They raised their glasses...clink'n'drink. As so often is the case, just when we are sure of what the next day will bring, it doesn't.

There surely are many surprises in this trip on the planet. However, the hangover next day wasn't one of them. Despite many causes for great joy, and an intense year of dedicated alcohol consumption, zz was a lowly and miserable human being on the morning after his Big Break. He slept through most of that day and night, then awoke early the next day...and found a smile splitting his face. With his newly found fortune came a burst of energy. Quickly up and in the shower, zz was singin' with gusto.

He had never been much interested in food, so skipping breakfast was nothing unusual. But skipping his morning Rumpunch! was unusual.

zz wandered into the backyard and lit up his three cherry pipe tobacco. He sat still and peacefully, a leaf on the river...while raging currents swirled below.

First up was the absence of pressure! Two days ago he had been balanced on the slippery slope of looming eviction, with few possessions to haul and nowhere to haul them. Now the magic wand had been waved! He had a job, income, and a place to live. He wasn't sure how much he would make, but Gravel Dr. Rasp had said he would be making about what a schoolteacher on the job for 25 years would make. "Not much," he had laughed, "but since it's just you, and rent free, you'll be OK." The rest of the details would follow in an e-mail, including the address of the house/radio station in a college town nearby.

It took hours for the disbelief and shock to fade. He spent the day wandering through his lost castle, staying awhile in each room to see what memories arrived.

The possibilities of the future eased the sting of eviction…

Returning to the backyard he sat as the sunset, and his imagination set to work. Disc jockey! What type of equipment? Broadcasting hours? Guests? Talk shows? Discussions? Feature local bands? Gravel mentioned there was no need to worry about advertising…and zz could create his own playlists; anything he wanted to explore, he could!

On and on his mind rambled, examining the wide range of changes in his personal life. What would his new place look like? What would he stock in his refrigerator? He smiled like a king, realizing he could get some long needed repairs on his old car. He felt again the disgrace of being a father and a grandfather with no money to buy the kids gifts for birthdays and Christmas; everyone around him had backed off, not sure what to do with a fallen father.

Lost in thought, zz carefully considered each of his three children and five grandkids. That first check would buy some belated but beautiful gifts.

On and on he went, like a surfer riding a beautiful wave. His mind went to the grandiose: maybe he would run the heater when he was cold, without sweating the bill. Or even order newspaper delivery! Perhaps he would take a little vacation! His favorite vacation? Get in the car, push the pedal, and make it up from there. Oh yes, the Open Road!

So happy was he in his speculation that he did not think it possible to feel any more joy and exhilaration, wonder and hope, than he did now. Yet as he lay there, basking in his newfound sunlight, another world overcame him…a world that made his fresh and profound joy seem like a Desert in which he traveled, seeking an Oasis.

Where were the browns, blacks, pinky-whites? The furrows, valleys, curves, and wet, warm caves? Where had the thunder over the tropical ocean gone, with ripping lightning bolts in its wake?

My God in Heaven, what about the Women?!?

What About the Women?

zz had long appreciated the complexity of women. Nothing in the world so drew his curiosity, so enthralled and perplexed him--each woman a universe of wonders and marvels. He wholeheartedly believed the world would have been a better place, and easier on both sexes, if females had been called "paradoxes" right from the start.

par·a·dox

1. A seemingly contradictory statement that may nonetheless be true: the paradox that standing is more tiring than walking.

2. One exhibiting inexplicable or contradictory aspects: "The silence of midnight, to speak truly, though apparently a paradox, rung in my ears" (Mary Shelley).

3. An assertion that is essentially self-contradictory, though based on a valid deduction from acceptable premises.

4. A statement contrary to received opinion.

5. Femininity: @ !

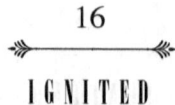

The next morning zz was up with the sunrise. The first thing he decided to do was join some dating sites. He had friends and family who had prospered with internet dating. His day-to-day routine had no interaction with women. He certainly wasn't going to meet anybody on the job, being the one and only employee in the building. All over the world more and more people were turning to the net to meet. Sad to say, in today's world of work, run by accountants and attorneys, even a simple flirtation could have severe career ramifications. However, casting the negative aside, net dating had many advantages.

By getting on the net he had the opportunity for a better introduction than in person; essays and test/question responses gave him more insight than a passing hello. He thought the process would be interesting. A few e-mails and phone calls ahead of meeting allows two people to develop some momentum, establish some common ground, and ease the pressure when meeting did occur.

Bottom line? There was nowhere in his day-to-day world where he would meet a woman. He had no interest in clubbing, or asking someone for a date in the broccoli section of the supermarket.

Where to get started? Which dating site to choose? He sat down at the computer, and started reading about many dating sites. He found customer reviews to be so helpful! He read, made notes, compared…

Research now done, zz was psyched for a couple of sites. Once in action, he found that dating sites take one through some tough philosophical trips. Right away, in filling out the profile, the top two questions were soul-searchers! Who are you, and what do you seek?

zz was in a quandary. In his mind, "who are you?" = "what have you got to offer?' Of course, every male in the world knows they can offer great sex, but beyond that...hmmmmmm...zz had to give it a hard look, and he saw that he wasn't such a good catch! Still...women...sex...mmmmm...

Having thought of sex, zz's mind wandered to the profile's question number 2: What did he want?

zz remembered a good joke that summed it up pretty well. From a female comedian: "There's 3-4 guys cruisin' along and they spot a woman walking down the street. They slow up the car for conversation, like "Howzzz it goin'?", or, "You're hot, baby!" She is given a few other heartfelt compliments, then smiles, and the guys ask her if she wants to get in the car and go for a cruise. "No way!" she says. They screech away. Now reverse it. Three or four women come by, flirt, and then ask the guy to get in the car. What does he say?"

"You bet!!!"

"That's the trouble with guys; they'll get in the car."

He also remembered something a friend had said; youth is the greatest aphrodisiac. For a while zz floated around in the lift of a dream about a town full of college students, and the delightful possibilities. He saw a stream of twenty somethings reflecting golden sunlight.

Such sweet dreams...all gliding by like childhood dreams of flying, or being invisible. Fortunately for zz that fantasy snapped shut, and Reality moved up to the forefront. He walked into the bathroom and took a long look into a full-length mirror.

It had always amused zz how men were so free to criticize women's bodies. He could not remember how many times he had sat with beer-bellied, wide-assed, unkempt men dissin' some woman because of small breasts, or 10 extra pounds. Pathetic!

IGNITED

Now add to the scene that same gut-slinging, broad-butted, balding, beer guzzler partnered up with a college student. What's wrong with that picture?

zz didn't drink beer, and didn't have much of a gut. He was still at high school weight, and had some quickness and agility left. But he was honest enough to realize a man of his years, with the gray hair, arthritis, decreasing eyesight, and wrinkles aplenty, might not be much of a catch for younger women. As this unsettling truth hit home, he was right back at Question 1: Who are you--what do you offer?

He moved into the living room, sitting in one of the few pieces of furniture left him when his wife moved out, his good old leather recliner. He leaned back, and set to thinking. Not much did he have to offer, he had to admit. He had just started a job, and had a ten-year-old car. There was no money in the bank, and he would be living in a radio station. In addition, he had many other flaws that had caused grief in his marriage, including his aversion to monogamy. What did he have to offer? That question had him stumped! He drifted off to sleep lost in a puzzle.

About 3 A.M., he awoke to an Answer: the Years, and what they brought to the Here and Now, were his strength. The Moment...that was his gift. He felt, in ways too profound for words, the shock and beauty of this revelation.

He stayed in the recliner for a couple more hours, now wide awake his thoughts churning. As the sun rose, so did he, moving through the house, too energized to sit. From moment to moment, room to room, sitting here, standing there, he wandered through the day, wondering if he could trust such a radical transformation! Could his age and accompanying wit be his greatest asset?

It had taken him 50 years to learn not to trust all his own

thoughts. So he decided to give it all a little more contemplation. He took a shower, had a hot drink, and sat down in his chair for a smoke. Nothing in his thinking changed or wavered, not even when he looked in the mirror. His experiences were etched across his face, but nowhere more than in his eyes. He leaned into the mirror, gazing into layer upon layer of depth, like looking from the mountain down into the valley.

That realization soon supplied another: he would like to see that same look in the eyes of a lover! She too would have the physical flaws of time on the planet, with the beauty of her experiences hidden like diamonds in the rough. Like zz, she would know that time is dwindling, each minute ever more precious.

zz moved to the backyard and eased into a lawn chair, basking in the warm sun. He closed his eyes and eased into his new vision. Women near zz's age had splendors impossible to possess in youth. One such was a seasoned view of men. Those who no longer appreciated men had migrated elsewhere. Those who did appreciate males had an awareness, a tolerance and understanding of men, free of useless hopes. They could say "Damn men!" with a smile. Women near zz's age had little time or energy for drama.

And sexually? How many women had told him they were astounded to find their passion and responsiveness multiplied by the years? That amazing change, along with the skills the years bring, had zz even more convinced! He was excited and energized by his newfound vision! He was going to build a dating future, and his foundation was set; he knew who he was, and what he sought.

Lyrics from the musical The Music Man said it well:

"No bright-eyed, blushing, breathless baby-doll baby,
Not for me
That kinda child ties knots no sailor ever knew
I prefer to take a chance on a more adult romance
No dewy young miss
Who keeps resisting all the time she keeps insisting!
No wide-eyed, wholesome innocent female
No sir
Why, she's the fisherman, I'm the fish you see?--PLOP!
I flinch, I shy, when the lass with the delicate air goes by
I smile, I grin, when the gal with a touch of sin walks in
I hope, and I pray, for a Hester to win just one more "A"
The sadder-but-wiser girl's the girl for me
The sadder-but-wiser girl for me"

The excitement was too much! zz could no longer sit still…he had to move! He hopped up and headed inside, realizing he hadn't eaten all day. He stopped by the stereo in the living room and started up some Ray Charles, then zipped to the kitchen. Moving to the music, he prepared some beans and guacamole, feeling so damn good!

As he cooked, ate and cleaned up, the surge toward an exciting future spurred his mind, riding up to what he had to offer. His main gift? The Moment. His funny and sunny disposition, ability to communicate, interesting job, and true love of women might appeal to some. With his retirement looking bleak, and little disposable income, he would be a poor fit with someone wanting a partner for the future. Neither would he be good for someone with resources, looking to enjoy theater, music, dining out, weekend getaways, or travel. He would never take money from a woman, so any woman that went out with him would be poor also. Few women would appreciate that!

During the day the music continued to play as zz packed and stacked boxes. Somehow, maybe just for the truth of it, realizing his circumstances gave him an ease and comfort with his situation. He was fine living a life of simple pleasures, and wouldn't mind meeting the same in a woman. Knowing he wasn't much of a long-term prospect for a relationship was fine also. It fit with a deep down opinion he held: relationships cooled passion. Domesticated love was not hot love.

Early in a relationship, lovemaking was fresh and steamy, full of exploration and joy. The time between dates was full of anticipation, with e-mails and phone calls tempting connections. Stuck in traffic? Filling out a form? Or any other daily aggravations that so often squeeze the spirit from life. Yet when he thought of his lover, maybe the last time they met, or a future date, the weight would disappear and he would have trouble keeping his feet on the ground.

Whenever he had been fortunate enough to have a lover, he found an extra special ingredient was the privacy. It was his, all his. zz would look around knowing no one knew, no friend or family member, coworker or stranger. He and his lover created a mutually enhancing Oasis in the desert and only they had the map.

Once a full time relationship set in, so did the introductions to friends and relatives, the attending mutual holidays, birthday parties, and weddings. Then discussions would revolve around arrangements on dishwashing and laundry, furniture matching carpet and walls, calendars, shared bills and purchases. Many believed that progression to be the natural evolution of a relationship, strands woven into the tapestry. A tapestry of priorities that included passion's strand, there among the other priorities. Most women his age were seeking their Last Great Relationship...but certainly not all.

zz remembered an article he read by Chelsea Chapman not long ago. In the article she pointed out some basic differences between American women and French women.
American women approach relationships in goal-oriented form. They have a list of what they want, and a clear vision of the type of relationship they seek. They seek known outcomes...total love or total rejection.

French women see romantic encounters more in terms of possibilities. Will this turn out to be a friend? Lover? A casual hello and goodbye? French women enjoy exploring without specific outcomes in mind...setting things in motion while entering the unknown.

zz was a dude lookin' for a French attitude.

About midnight, following dinner and a shower, zz felt no fatigue. He returned to his computer knowing he had his thoughts together on the first question. But now he found the next question tough, too. The body type he sought? Americans were indoctrinated by all forms of media to believe tall, blonde, thin young women with big ones rock! Hear the testosterone give a standing ovation!

From high school through college graduation, and on into his professional life, zz was fascinated by the study of history. He had studied with great interest the early 1900s, when women en masse began getting paying jobs, the fashion industry exploded. At the first international fashion conference in Paris in the 1920s, designers and buyers met and exchanged ideas, and orders for goods. America was the one and only country that brought back fashions suited only to tall thin women, an enduring and demonic legacy!

Long ago zz had observed how hard women were on themselves and their own bodies. Hypercritical! They scoured themselves minutely in the mirror, finding flaws even where there were none. That angst with the body could make aging, like so many other things, much harder on women than men. It was one of zz's lifelong goals to rent every billboard, buy all advertising in newspapers and magazines, and take every TV and radio commercial in America for an entire day. That whole day he would broadcast that women are beautiful in every shape, size and age. He was a man on a mission, and if he couldn't get his day of advertising, he would have to let as many women as possible know in person how fine they were!

zz thought it over, realizing his own imperfections included some extra pounds, he felt in his heart it was his duty to take on the fashion industry's prejudice! In order to win, he'd get beyond the thin!

Then and there he had his answer, and wrote it out: Body Type: Any.

Over the next few weeks internet dating was only a slice of zz's busy days. He had to clean up the old place, move and unpack, and prepare for a new career. Still, throughout all, his attention to women was steadfast.

Putting thought into action, changing prejudice to acceptance, isn't easy, but zz was willing to work. Every day he was on the net, cruising many sites, seeking photos of women 50-70. Looking in his own mirror, as well as at the pics of advancing age, he found himself humming along with the Bonnie Raitt song, "Nick of Time." Even though we know the lines and wrinkles are part of a natural way, they still aren't easy to look at Today.

So zz had to freshen and reawaken his mind, transcend brainwashing and deception. Before long he began to see the marks of character that time had made on a body in fifty or sixty years as something unique and beautiful. His eyes and desires found harmony with his newly realized revelation: age has unique beauty, with the possibility of exciting exploration ahead. Fall, rich with the colors of the changing Earth, awaits the next spring as eagerly as a child.

So it goes! Man, 57, lively and agile of mind and body, looking for the same in a woman, 50-70. Body type: Any. Seeking to date, not a relationship...someone to go out with, not someone to come home to.

L e a v i n g
L i m b o

"After all these years, I see that I was mistaken
about Eve in the beginning; it is better to live outside
the Garden with her than inside it without her."

-"Extracts from Adam's Diary", Mark Twain

He had the me, and he had the you...what dating site should
zz move through? Of sites zz researched, straight and erotic, he
believed OK Cupid to be the finest. As usual, there is an essay
introduction (which zz reads very carefully!). In addition, OK uses
a compatibility rating based on a series of tests and questions that
prove to be very illuminating. The areas covered include Lifestyle,
Religion, Dating, Ethics and SEX. zz was sure most men hit the sex
surveys first, and he was no exception.

zz was in a perpetual state of amazement with the growth
of his sexual appetite and fantasies as he had aged! Why hadn't
somebody told him about it when he was in high school? If he
had known his interest in sex would still be seeking an apex as
he neared 60...wow! He would have viewed aging and the elderly
much differently. The only way he was slowing up was by taking
two or three hours each time he made love, instead of the 30-45
minutes he took in his twenties. Foreplay galore and staying power
for sure...mmmmmmm. And his imagination matched the explosion
in his body; for most of his life zz's fantasies had one general
direction, but now they were exploding in so many directions so
rapidly he could scarcely find time to keep track of them, much less
indulge them!

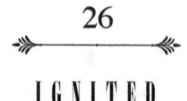

Although it was a frenetic month, moving and learning a new job, zz kept up the search. He spent hours reading and studying profiles, trying to imagine situations and compatibility, seeing what each person brought to the table. Checking the pics of course, but always keeping in mind some advice from a Robert Palmer song, that a pretty face is not necessarily the sign of a pretty heart.

About the same time zz investigated dating he reconnected with a friend who had lost his wife to cancer while zz's marriage crumbled. They had known each other since they were 16. Despite zz's migration through six states, including nine years in Hawaii, they had stayed tight. As they had promised in high school, and throughout the years: womb to tomb; birth to earth. But death and divorce had driven them to separate caves.

It was a surprise for Howie when he stopped by to find zz about packed and ready to go. After some heartfelt hellos, they headed for the fridge, poured some Rumpunch!, grabbed some chips and dip, sat down, clinked glasses, and began a conversation that would last hours.

Howie was delighted with the emergence of their mutual friend, Gravel Rasp, and all the positive changes for zz. He told some hows and whats of his wife's illness, passing, and his gradual recuperation. Eventually a lifelong favorite topic came to the forefront: Women.

Howie was about ready for some companionship, so zz told him about his move to internet dating. Right away they discovered a difference in approaches.

zz enjoyed a gradual e-mailing and phone call trail. He liked learning about lives: jobs, kids, hobbies, habits, hopes and dreams. Doors and windows to worlds unknown to him were opened, and he appreciated the varied perspectives. Also, the information helped him project some measure of compatibility. Howie said to him it seemed that the whole point was meeting. Why spend so much time and energy without knowing if there was attraction?

zz also suspected his view differed from most. He wasn't expecting a magical meeting, or an instantaneous spark setting off fireworks. He sort of expected to walk a liking into a loving. zz wasn't much for first impressions, and a good thing too; he remembered a wonderful love affair that began with her throwing up on the first date.

You never know what!

Soon after Howie and zz reconnected, zz was ready for a trip to the ocean. His house was in order, and he knew as much as he could know about running a radio station. He had some down time as paperwork for licensing was still in the process.

Ever since his transformation, zz's head had been a whirling dervish. As wonderful as his many changes were, he still felt overwhelmed, Being by the ocean had always helped zz sift, sort, and settle. An idle drive and a day near the sea was part of what he needed!

He had another special reason: Naneeka. They had exchanged a few notes during the past month, but she was reluctant to meet… distance was the deterrent. Even though they were only an hour apart, Naneeka hoped for someone nearby. However, zz had maintained interest, and they had continued communication.

Naneeka

"I would rather be a beggar and single than a queen and married."

-Queen Elizabeth

Ten years before Naneeka met zz, she was on the verge of asking her husband for a divorce. She liked and loved him, but passion had disappeared from their partnership and she was no longer willing to settle. The decision had not been a quick one. In her case it was Time Fortified; for months she imagined a new life, and found her desire increasing daily. At last, she knew with certainty it was time to make the move. Little did she know that her Exit was about to be blocked by the Entrance of a brand new player: Cancer.

The very week Naneeka was going to let her man know it was goodbye, he gave her the sharp surprise: he had about five years to live. When the shock and tears passed, she looked at the decades they had spent together, and the two sons so strongly resembling him. Looking at her children cleared her mind, and she knew her duty; she would stay by her man and see it through.

That she did...and five years became seven. No need to delve into those seven years, a book in itself. Following his death, she concentrated on her family, friends and work for almost three years. Then one morning she awoke, and took her cup of coffee out to the garden. Suddenly laughing aloud, she realized her decade old desire had resurfaced; she was ready, able and more than willing to meet some men.

It was to be pure exploration; Naneeka was so far removed

from days of a happy relationship that her hopes, dreams and a very staunch grip on reality drove her curiosity. Her desires were awaiting a form.

Since she had no idea of who and what she wanted, she was in no rush for a relationship. She did know that no man in her life interested her romantically. Going with the flow of the day, and with a couple of friends encouraging her, she decided to try online dating.

Being 5' 10" tall, black, with a long full body, she is the Amazon queen: tall, strong, and bold. Her eyes full and round, light brown dancing with hazel flecks near the iris. They are intense, piercing in perception, yet gentle and warm when she spoke. She wore a green sleeveless blouse that revealed well-defined arms, with a slice of generous cleavage. The blouse dropped over a pair of jeans, which she filled with vigor. There is no queenly behavior in this Lady. She is down to earth, carrying the aura of a pioneer: resolute, concerned, balanced…a staunch disposition. She had a troubling amount of mirth riding in her eyes, a mix of mischief and good humor. How could she not be flattered by the number of men contacting her? She barely had time to respond to all.

When zz first e-mailed her she sent him packing...too much distance, she said! But he had it in his heart and mind to pursue, with the special added ingredient so new to zz, given him by his aging: patience!

So he waited a few weeks for spring, and e-mailed her, saying he was coming into town. Might she like to meet? She responded with a few concerns, one being the difference in height! She didn't like shorter men! zz fired right back, "I played and coached basketball for 35 years. I've said it before, and I'll say it again. You can be bigger than me, but you better not act bigger than me!"

Her reply soon arrived; if zz was coming to town, let her know...a walk and talk might be fun.

Hachachacha!

They met on a university campus in front of the library, on a fine spring day, and took a walk alongside a stream running through campus. Naneeka moved with ease and athleticism; their conversation moved gracefully through many subjects: job likes and dislikes, politics, childhood experiences, prior relationships, children. They walked a mile or so out the creek and then started back, stopping at a bench overlooking a bridge ducks quacking through the underpass.

Each step of the way, and there on the bench, zz tried not to be too obvious about his urge to stare at her body. Her dark skin had a glow, a shimmer about it...almost as if it moved like a slowly running river. She soaked up sunshine like a kid eating ice cream. The color was soft, thick...a combination of fertile soil and mahogany. Her legs were like tree trunks: straight and strong. Her breasts and ass were full like bursting fruit.

He tried to keep his eyes on hers, but often found them wandering! She observed him with sweetened eyes, as they smiled and chatted and chatted and smiled. Looking back at it later, zz wondered where he got his nerve...maybe it was the quacking ducks! But he leaned in for a kiss, and she leaned right back...time stopped for a while, as the kiss lingered...that kiss led to two or three more...

She pulled back first, and gave him a funny look...that mischievous glint in her eyes heightened. They stood up, and walked on...all the way back to his car. Then, like two teens at the drive in movies, they climbed in the back seat. First zz gave her a shoulder and neck massage, working his hands inside her sleeveless blouse. They necked and petted for a half hour, occasionally having to straighten up quickly when someone came through the parking lot.

The next date was set for the following week at her house, which was very close to the university.

Caramba!

May I Feel,
Said He

---

may i feel said he
(i'll squeal said she
just once said he)
it's fun said she

(may i touch said he
how much said she
a lot said he)
why not said she

(let's go said he
not too far said she
what's to far said he
where you are said she)

may i stay said he
(which way said she
like this said he
if you kiss said she

may i move said he
is it love said she)
if you're willing said he
(but your're killing said she

but it's life said he
but your wife said she
now said he)
ow said she

(tiptop said he
don't stop said she
oh no said he
go slow said she

cccome? said he
ummn said she)
you're divine! said he
(you are Mine said she)

-ee cummings

In the hour drive to her house zz enjoyed his pipe and some inspired silence...living the dream. He arrived on the edge of sunset. Her home was at the top of a hill very near the university. The two-story house was 50-60 years old, and had wood galore: doors, floors, stairway, bookshelves...the rich forest brown scent of wood permeated her home. The windows were everywhere and large; plants thrived in every room. They picked up a glass of red wine on the way to her small backyard. Since her house was at the top of a little hill, the view of the sunset was perfect Roses clustered in one corner of the yard; at the other side of the yard was a hot tub sheltered by a small redwood roof with matching walls and deck. zz's imagination was swimming.

They sat in lawn chairs watching the oncoming night, sharing some wine and smoke. Again conversation flowed with ease and laughter.

"Life is full of crossroads, isn't it?" Naneeka ventured. "And so often it comes down to a decision, a fork in the road."

"Yep!" said zz. "Sometimes that decision is yours to make, and sometimes it's made for you. Sometimes it's a combo pack."

"How do you mean?" Naneeka asked.

"Well," zz countered," like in your situation. You were on the threshold of leaving your husband, and living the new life…your decision made. Then Fate strikes and he has cancer: a chosen road now has that fork. Your decision is reversed; you were ready to go, but stayed. Who knows what the last 7 years would have held had you left?"

Naneeka spoke in a low, cool voice, "There were times when my imagination would keep me afloat. One day I would pretend I was on a world tour, flying through Europe, Asia, or Africa. Along the way I met a fellow traveler, from Hawaii. We would fly to his home on the ocean and…" she laughed heartily…" get Native."

"Another time," she continued, "I was taking a walk near my house when a couple drove up in a car and asked for directions. As I explained they jumped from their car, pushed me in the back seat, kidnapped me and took me to their home, where I was forced to do many TERRIBLE things!" More laughter.

She laughed again, and put her hand on his turned to zz and stared straight into his eyes. "Speaking of decisions being made by us, or for us, and their sometimes intertwined trails, how about you?"

"How do you mean?" said zz, observing the mischievous twinkle in her eye with some distrust.

"You wanted something different during your marriage, and when the road forked…mistress, or none…you had a mistress. Your choice. Then down the road your wife finds out, and leaves you. No choice in that fork for you!"

zz laughed! "Well, we've both got our forks…let's eat!"

They cut some roses from the bushes out back, and went on a tour of her home, including the remains of a clubhouse shared by her two sons. Her boys were brilliant scholars and down home jocks; photos of their football and rugby playing days from high school and college hung here and there.

Naneeka and zz returned to the living room and sat down on a sofa near the fireplace and snuggled for a while, then made their way upstairs to her bedroom. zz carried the roses. As he climbed the stairs, he noticed her entire house had the feel of an antique store...well used and ripe with character.

She pulled back the covers and they lay down on crisp white sheets. zz placed the roses on her nightstand, and eased his way against her, face to face. They hugged, kissed, and fondled as zz slowly undressed them, joy rising in his heart and sex with each unveiling. He had her roll over on her belly, and got on his knees between her legs.

Opening her, he took a deep breath, inhaling her wetscent rising to him, and reached for one of the red roses. He put his nose to the rose, again inhaling deeply and slowly.

He inhaled, caught her scent again, and placed the rose at the top of her spine, just under her short brown hair. He moved along her spine, swishing the rose slowly from side to side as he traced downward. As he moved the rose, petals fell off and rolled across her body, falling down to the sheets, red splashes on white linen.

He reached for another rose, and started where her left thigh met her sweetly rounded bottom, again swishing side to side, petals tumbling as he stroked. For the next half hour he massaged her from foot to head, until she was lost, in a sort of delirium.

As he rolled her over onto her back, she wrapped those endless legs around him and tried to pull him into her. He moved his thighs inside hers and pushed her open, and put his hands on her wrists and held her down. He would not enter her, but leaned down and again kissed her. This kiss was unlike any they had shared so far... she pushed her mouth ferociously into his, even taking little bites at his lips and tongue. He pulled back, and laughed. "Easy Tiger," he crooned in her ear, "not so fast."

He moved to the foot of the bed, between her feet, and took another rose from the table. Beginning where her thighs met her sex (which had gone untouched!), he drew short brushstrokes down her legs, and back up. He again moved his knees inside her upper thighs, opening and pinning her, and moved another rose across her belly, and up between her breasts. He had just started on her neck when she spasmed, closing her legs tight around his, hands locked around his wrists, her head whipping side to side as she emitted a lowslung growl...

When she was finished he continued drawing the rose across her, waiting to the end to touch her breasts and sex. Taking a rose in each hand, he started on her breasts by moving the rose in circles around the base of her breasts, then the middle, just brushing her areolas. At last her nipples. He let the roses sit still on the tip of each breast, their feathery texture cool and rough against her burning nipples. Then his hands began moving side to side, each rose like a pendulum that swings across her nipple, sits in midair a moment, before brushing her again. She begins to laugh and groan, mixing the two, and her thighs again clenched his... ohhhhhhh!!!!!!

Waiting for her tremors to spread, like ripples on the pond, he could not help noticing her face looked refreshed, renewed... it was as if the years dropped away, and she was again in her twenties. Even those words fall short; it took zz's breath away... indescribable moment of beauty.

Picking up another rose he headed for that tight and sopping sex. Her juices shone on both of her thighs, soaking into the sheets and rose petals beneath her. He again swirled the rose in circles, avoiding her sex, brushing her belly and thighs. Taking a single rose he traced her sex lips...several times going the length of her sex and back again, keeping the pressure light but steady...finally he attacked her quivering clit.

He took the rose and whapped it side to side across that throbbing button, as much hitting it as stroking it. She emitted a symphony of sounds...gasps, grunts, moans, groans and laughter building toward orgasm, until her hips shot off the mattress as if rocket launched, and an aieeeeeeeeee echoed off the walls...

Tossing the rose aside he wrapped his arms around her, pulling her to him and kissing her with patient passion, waiting for her tremors to ease. She opened her eyes, pulled back from the kiss and pulled his head tightly to her chest.

She pulled his head back up for a kiss with one hand, and grabbed his pounding sex, enormously swollen, with the other, bringing it to her sex. He eased inside her. He slowly pushed until he was all the way inside, then stopped moving. Again her body tightened and another tremor shook her as she hooked her nails in his back. Ouch!

He sat still as she pushed up and down his shaft in a rapid frenzy to another shuddering cum. Again he thrust the last of his very thick, full veined, circumcised, purple plum-tipped 8" cock into her, and she began another kind of moan, tossing her head side to side, as if she might actually lose her mind. He left it there, fully embedded, loving the feel of this once roaring big cat, now moaning in surrender.

He whispered in her ear, "feel it...is it splitting you wide? Can you feel the veins throbbing? Is the tip up in your belly, pushing? Feel my balls--their heat against you?"

"You're so slippery and hot on me"...on and on he went as she shook again...beginning a series of spiraling explosions...his sex so completely penetrating her, pinning her to the bed, was almost too much; too many sensations landing at once!

He kept his weight on her, pinning her down. Unable to do more than twist her hips a little made his cock seem even more enormous, each part more pronounced. Her impressions wavered wildly, from feeling as if he might actually split her open, to

39

believing this fullness within her was her slice of Heaven. Her string of orgasms reached a crescendo, and slowly subsided. He eased his legs and arms, moving his weight from her.

It took her a moment to realize she could move freely. When she did she attacked his sex with vigor. He sat unmoving between her legs as she ground her hips up and down, her pussy in a wild frenzy, sliding over and squeezing with all her might this monster that she had feared would devour her moments ago.

Her body shook in a different kind of orgasm; this started in her sex like a rock hitting the surface of a pond, then rippling out in every direction. She felt as if every cell in every part of her was coming. She had never heard herself bellow when coming like she had that night; exhausted and finished she collapsed back to the crisp white sheets.

He gently withdrew; she gasped and moaned as he slipped out of her. He again rolled her over. This time she complied easily... no resistance left. Looking at the strewn rose petals, on sheets now soaked with her juices, he pulled two pillows under her hips, and moved in tight behind her, spreading her thighs with his.

"What are you doing?" she asked with some trepidation.

He leaned forward, and swiftly entered her from behind. For some reason her first instinct was to try and crawl forward, away from that organ. But he grabbed her hair to hold her still, and started easing slowly in and out, while moving his hands to her hips, holding her immobile...even though she had little energy left to move.

"Did you think that was fucking?" he crooned with a low growl, as he slowly pushed to the depth, and back again. "No...that was me letting you play!"

His thrusts picked up speed, depth, changing angles and intensity as he whispered in her ear, "MY turn!"

Since he first began making love zz had a peculiar condition. When he was young he had worried, and considered it sort of an affliction. Once he came to the edge of an orgasm two or three times, and stopped just before coming, he could not come that night no matter how long or how hard he tried. His orgasm had to wait for the next day, when he would forget all foreplay, enter quickly, pumping furiously and come in five minutes or less.

Of course the blessing of his "condition" was that on nights he did not come, he could go and go, remaining relentlessly erect... occasionally women who had begged for him to enter them ended up begging just as hard for him to stop.

Being a gentleman, he would of course give them what they desired...

Such a night it was for Naneeka, who would never ever have believed it was possible, pleading with a man to stop doing her, for fear one more orgasm would make her lose her mind.

They slept on sheets reddened by petals soaked in sweat and sex juices. The next morning her took her missionary style, locked in a kiss; they quickly and mutually came in a frenzy...

Later that day he sent her a poem...

Rosy Repose

Jungle Rain
Petals, blood red
make a trail
'cross crinkled sheets...

soft, silky
red roses,
pounding percussion;
rhythms of the jungle

each petal's heat
absorbs the beat;
moistened red's
been freshly fed

tiger's breathing scorches
moving through the brush;
congos, burning torches
make the heart rush
neck and breasts and belly stroked
calves, thighs...little sex stoked;
wet and wild, pleasure nearly pain,
petals soaked with jungle rain.

About an hour later, she responded.

Showersing

Gently stinging pats
punctuating the pleasures
of rolling 'round with you
on crisp white sheets.

a stirring deep inside
sending ripples into waves of joy
igniting my Venus to your Mars
on crisp white sheets

but today showers are
dancing off the grass and
running down the window panes
singing reflections of intertwined frolickers
on crisp white sheets.

As they were equally enamored and eager for the next encounter, they arranged to meet the next week. During a fun and spicy phone call zz came up with a scenario, asking Naneeka if she would like to try. As he spun out his plot to her on the phone he was pleasantly surprised when her breathing took on that ragged, swiftshallow sound of her just before coming. And then she did, exploding into his ear as he ambled easily on with promises of new adventures, arriving with tomorrow's full moon.

Come on Up

"Any time you got nothing to do – and lots of time to do it – come on up."

-Mae West

When he arrived she met him at the door, dressed as he had requested, in a full-length black silk negligee. Later she would wonder why he made that request; he removed it not long after his arrival. First he stepped into the room and into her, wrapping his arms around her, pulling her tightly to him, mouths locked...zz then stepped back and his eyes dined awhile. He had her walk across the room and back again twice, watching her body move with the silk flowing. He kissed her again; during that kiss he untied the sash holding up her gown and it fell to the floor.

Although he would have been happy staring the rest of the day, zz moved in behind Naneeka and put his arms around her waist, placing his hands on her belly. His erection pushed against the soft insides of her thighs. He pushed his knees into the back of hers, causing her to fall back against him. He moved his hands to cup her breasts firmly, while he gently massaged her nipples with the thumb and forefinger of each hand. Her ass now rested on his bent knees and thighs. She scooted up and rubbed back and forth against the shaft of his sex as that grrrring moan picked up volume and tempo until she came, pushing back hard against him.

He then pulled a black silk sash from his pocket and blindfolded her. Immediately, she found that the blindfold was causing strange sensations. Being unable to see and read his face

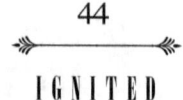

made her wonder what he thinking, doing. When he told her he was admiring the view, she blushed...she heard him walk behind her, his belt being unbuckled, and his pants removed, tossed to the floor. She heard the brush-rustle of his shirt and boxers coming off. Her head and sex began pounding and a tremor shook her legs. The feel of his eyes upon her and being unable to see his expression heightened her vulnerability...she felt the need to be protected!

He placed his hands on her hips while guiding her across the living room to the high back of the sofa. He moved a hand to her neck and gently bent her forward over the back of the sofa. Her long legs and so fine ass met the top of the sofa perfectly; her head and arms rested easily on the cushions. He put his feet inside hers and spread her wider, while cupping each tiny cheek of her ass with a hand, pulling her open. He then dropped to his knees, moving his hands to her calves. He massaged each leg from calf to waist, returning to her ass, massaging and opening her as he moved his lips to the base of her spine, giving her a long warm kiss. He then ran his licking tongue down the opening of her ass, swirling side to side across her asshole, and down the outside of the lips of her sex.

By this time Naneeka was thrashing side-to-side and pushing back toward him; he firmly grabbed her ass and held her down while continuing to move his mouth over her inflamed pussy. After her sexlips were so swollen and throbbing she feared they would explode, he penetrated her with his tongue. She moaned a drawn out aaaaaaaaagh! Increasing the grip and pressure on her ass with his hands he upped the tempo of his tonguethrusts, and again she orgasmed...succumbing and slouching into the sofa.

He placed his right hand on his cock, and lifted it to her sex, running the knob up and down her opening. Her body tensed and tightened and her desire, already past boiling, began steaming. She tried to wriggle her way back onto him, but he put his left hand on her spine and held her still as he continued to tease her with his hot plum. At last zz slowly pushed in the knob, and just as slowly moved back, developing a slow easy tempo. It wasn't too long before she cried out another cum...this one despite herself and her frustration...put it all in!!

Again zz waited, enjoying her pouting and impatience. He pulled her up to a standing position, put his hands on her waist and guided her to the stairs. He had her climb the stairs ahead of him, moving closely behind her, preventing even a stumble. He was captivated by the ripple each movement made across her body; this time the growl arose from his chest...tiger in the moist.

As she reached the top of the stairs, he put a hand between her legs and inserted two fingers, both penetrating and lifting her. He had her walk to her room with his fingers in her...another way to feel the pulse of her movements. They reached the edge of the bed and he paused, softly kissing her shoulders and neck.

He turned her around for a squeeze and a kiss, then lowered her back onto the bed, helping her to move her head to her pillow. "Hold still" he told her, and then went to the bathroom for a cup of water. He returned to the bedroom and eased her into a spread-eagled position. Again using the blindfold to his favor, he moved around the bed, dipping his fingers in the water and then dropping it here and there on her. After she gasped and wiggled, he would put his hot mouth on her and lick off the water.

Most of the time he played with water and kisses she laughed. There were some oooooos and ahhhhhs, but more than anything some rib-shaking laughter. "Oh Lord!" she said more than once, "I am having such a wonderful time!'"

The laughter and lovin' ended past midnight, when zz had to make the hour drive home as there was an electrician coming early in the morning.

They began meeting about once a week; neither one had much more time available. Each time they met, zz picked a different one of her five senses to feature; after they had run through all five, he switched the order and started again.

The love affair lasted almost over a year; Naneeka then met a man who lived nearby. She was powerfully attracted, and felt that she was ready to pursue him exclusively. She and zz had always been softly blunt with each other. The very first date Naneeka had made it clear that more than time and distance stopped them from having a long-term relationship. She had plans to travel the world upon retirement, and zz's lack of "resources" would make traveling together impossible.

The friendship they built outlasted the love affair; they continued to communicate regularly by internet and phone, and meet occasionally for a warm drink and warmer conversation.

Sweet Puberty

"The only thing I am unable to resist is temptation."
-Oscar Wilde

For the next couple of weeks zz was looking back at his life, thinking of some crucial fork in the road decisions, and how things had gone…and how they might have been. At one point he got on the trail of his sexuality. Funny how he had left the starting gates early, then hit a long, slow stretch. He noticed a parallel. When he had lived to fit in, to get along, he had been bottled up in many areas…including sex. When breaking free of convention his spirit, and sex life, soared.

When he was younger, about 6th grade he met a friend who showed him a whole other way to travel. It was the way of the gypsy, free of rules and existence. zz had eagerly jumped on the wagon with his new friend. Immediately Life developed colors and angles that were new, fun and electric! The tight association with his friend lasted about three years, when zz jumped off the wagon.

His sexual life had suffered for sure, but a more subtle and insidious effect took place; by jumping off that wagon zz settled for established boundaries, and tried to be very good with them. There was an absence of wellness of fit!

zz felt he had left his friend out of fear. It was too wild and uncertain a ride, never knowing what was around the next corner. Now, looking back, he believed had he stayed on the ride he may have let himself out of the box…perhaps had another career, maybe made a living in some form of entertainment…paint, sing, write. Who knows? But it was about that time his personality had taken a turn, and he had buried some powerful interests and dreams in order to Fit In. A creative side just disappeared. And this was for sure: his sex life would have been an ongoing fireworks show had he kept up that exploration!

zz couldn't remember if his erotic imagination or puberty came first. When he was 10 years old he played some games to fill the dead time in school. He would see how long he could hold his breath. He tried to move objects with his mind, like getting pencils to roll across the desk. But his favorite was trying to make girls' clothes disappear. He worked long and hard on that one, closing his eyes and concentrating with a fury to see the Glories.

In sixth grade he made a friend who changed his life forever: Ray Marcer. Ray was the guide taking zz somewhere zz wanted to go badly, while clueless on how to get there. They were in the same school, but zz really got to know him through a paper route. After school they would gather with other paperboys to get the papers, fold and rubber band them, and off to deliver. Paperboys were all encouraged to get new subscribers, but Ray had his own system. Like other carriers he would canvas the neighborhoods, signing up new customers. However, he rarely reported new customers to the newspaper. The paper thought he had 55 customers when in fact he had over 100. The rest of us made about $35.00 a month: Ray made over $500. $500 a month for an 11 year old. Zowie!

One day a rogue customer called the paper to inquire about his account, and Ray was soon dismissed, after crime had very much paid.

Ray had two older brothers in high school who had taught him more than he needed to know. He hosted a birthday party one

Friday evening, supervised by his brothers. He turned it into a dance party for 40: 20 boys, including zz, and 20 girls.

The patio was covered with wax beads, smashed into the concrete, which made a slick dancing surface. They Chubby Checker twisted the night away...a few hours of dancing, with some hugs and kisses exchanged in the shadows...zz spent a good amount of time in the shadows.

Ray also took zz to a swim party at a girl's house on a fine summer afternoon; her parents were at work. There was a huge swimming pool, complete with two diving boards. During the course of the afternoon, several couples moved to chaise lounges on a wood deck, gone into kissing and heavy petting. That was the first time zz ever saw the feminine form nude, and the sheer joy nearly paralyzed him. :)

One night during the summer before 7th grade zz was staying the night at Ray's, and his parents dropped them off at a movie, *West Side Story*. Ray had arranged for a couple of girls to meet them there; they sat up high in the dark shadows of the balcony, necking and petting. The beauty zz was with (7th grader), removed her bra. For much of the movie he reveled in breasts...

At 11:00 P.M. the movie ended and their dates were picked up by The Parents. Standing at the curb outside the theater, zz said, "Looks like your Mom and Dad aren't here." Ray informed zz he'd purposefully mislead his parents, who were going to be out very late that night, telling his parents zz's parents were picking them up.

Soooooo cool!! Out near midnight, and just 12-years-old, walkin' the streets. They took a shortcut through downtown, a long, long alley between rows of business buildings, all connected as one. It was sorta fun, in that creepyscary kind of way, among the shadowed steel and glass, with iron rung ladders and trash cans against stained brick walls, and cats skittering about the crates and cardboard.

When they were about halfway down that long, long alley a car came in at the opposite end. It came fast down the narrow space and both boys had to jump as it zipped past. The driver was a teenager smoking a cigarette--he yelled, "Fuck you!"

Immediately Ray yelled "Fuck YOU!!"

The car screeched to a halt, and began backing up...zz's eyes opened three miles wide in disbelief and stark fear, staring at Mad Ray. Looking left and right he saw no exit; the office buildings were like canyon walls. No way he could outrun the car, or the teens inside. He almost passed out as the car backed up in rapid reverse. When it stopped beside them, they saw four teenagers, all smoking cigs and looking highly pissed off.

"Who said that?" the driver demanded. Before zz could blurt out "Nobody!", his crazy friend stepped to the car and said, "Me."

zz nearly threw up in wonderment, staring at Ray with his mouth wide open and total panic gripping his heart. A fast move by the driver started things in motion. Cigarette blazing, he shoved open the car door, put one foot on the ground, leaned out and popped Ray straight in the mouth. Faster than the driver and maybe even lightning, Ray grabbed the car door and slammed it on the driver's leg three times: BamBamBam!!!

With a banshee howl the driver leaped from the car and advanced on Ray, trying to kick him between the legs with some nasty sharp-toed boots, but Ray retreated too fast for the kicks to land. Then, like a cat of the jungle, Ray jumped into the driver and corralled him in a headlock, proceeding to smash him in the face a few times. The three guys in the car stared incredulously as Ray said, "I've had enough, if you have..."

The guy garbled out an OK, through split lips, blood, and

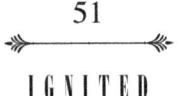

maybe some displaced teeth, clambering into the car and zooming off. And zz wasn't even dead!

When they reached the end of the alley, they rounded the corner and sat down on a bus bench. As zz breathed a humongous sigh of relief, Ray started to cry. He cried for quite some time.

More and more girls became part of the time they spent together. Although he did not yet "go all the way," zz learned his way around necking and petting. He was treated to the sight, touch and smell of many girls in various passionate poses.

zz knew he had been far more curious and eager to explore girls than nearly any guy he knew. But at this time, he also learned that somehow through the years, a border, a boundary had been established. Parents? Church? School? Conscience?

Despite a lot of encouragement from the opposite sex, zz was not comfortable moving into sexual intercourse, drinking, or other forms of advanced recreation.

Hanging with Ray had brought him many wonderful adventures, but Ray was now living in another universe. 14-years-old, and heading to the beach to surf with his brothers, gambling, guzzling beer, and even driving the car once in awhile! He was moving too fast for zz. After all, Ray carried condoms!

Looking back, zz often wondered why he had backed off. Here he was, over 50 years old, and still had not crossed the borderline, not truly let go. So many buried passions, fantasies.

Every once in a while zz hears of Ray from old acquaintances; tidbits floating in the wind. And the wind sings songs of Ray ridin' the range astride a mighty horse.

Me Tarzan, You Jane?

"Sex is emotion in motion."
-Mae West

It was that summer before 9th grade zz had his first introduction to dominant/submissive sexuality, and it captured his mind. He saw a movie where a teenage girl in San Francisco was kidnapped and taken to Candlestick Park. The kidnapper was apprehended just after he forced the girl to disrobe. The scene where she is forced to strip to her bra and panties set zz afire.

Another summer afternoon, visiting a bookstore downtown, he had a look at a magazine, sneaking it from the adult section and hiding it behind a book while devouring. In part of the story a man breaks into a home, forces a woman onto a table, pulls up her dress while pulling off her panties, and then performs oral sex until her resistance breaks into a bursting orgasm. There was furious masturbation to those scenes that summer.

If zz had known the trials and tribulations, heartaches and guilt looming ahead, blossoms of the rooted seed involving such sexual arisings, he might not have had so much fun.

In his marriage of 25 years the sex was domesticated before two or three years passed...harbored among the daily storms. However, whenever they did find time to enter the wild waters, it was inviting, exciting. She was a Brownskinned Beauty from Mexico, uniquely sensitive and sensuous. Her skin had the scent of rain and sun mingling on rich earth. How zz loved her touch, and touching her!

Yet she and zz differed in imagination, and that, along with many of zz's unorthodox ways, helped create a widening chasm over the years. In the gloom and doom year following the break up of his marriage, zz decided the world should be divided into two sexual categories: Literal and Figurative. Neither is better than the other; people can belong to both...the sex is just as hot on either side. He saw it more as a difference in approach.

The Literal Lovers are rich in sensual stimulation. The sight of their lover, exchanged touches, and the ensuing sounds, smells and tastes drive their passion. If they wander to the wild, it would be to the visual: porn movies, nude beaches, Playboy, and strip clubs.

The Figurative Folk intertwine imagination with sex. Many of the figurative, zz included, had an analytical brain that wouldn't shut up. No meditation, medication, or inhalation therapy could derail it. However, zz had found the joining of a lover and imagination silences that logical, linear lobe; imagination freed frees action from analysis! A lot of figurative frolicking takes place in that world known as Kink.

The combination of his family legacy, his inherent belief in social justice, the Women's Liberation Movement of the 1960/70s, and Primeval genetics brought quite a cacophony to zz's sexual harmony.

zz was born in a hardworking, physically/mentally/emotionally tough part of the U.S.A, Ohio near the West Virginia border, in a coal mining town. In that world men were the head of the household, no questions asked. Yet head of the house didn't mean tyrant. Men believed they were more capable of making a living than women. They took it as duty to protect, provide and care for their women. It was a very rough form of chivalry. In zz's household his Mom was tough as a rock and never disrespected or shut down in any way. But if it came to a tough or controversial decision, Pop made the call, and that was that.

As zz grew up, Social Change swept the nation, with long overdue verdicts of social justice delivered to many groups, including women. He was a fan of the changes. When he said, "I do," he believed marriage was an equal partnership, where decisions should be made by two acting as one. In zz's case, that turned out to be a road to hell paved with good intentions.

If we are fortunate enough to live a long life and tumble to some understanding of ourselves, we cannot ignore the Primal. Carl Jung said each person contains within themselves a blueprint of all symbols important to humanity. When zz started looking for a woman, he had come to the conclusion that his sexual nature desired a submissive woman, but more importantly he felt it primal in his heart and soul: man was born to lead woman; me Tarzan, you Jane.

Me Jane, Where's Tarzan?

"I do not want to be the leader. I refuse to be the leader. I want to live darkly and richly in my femaleness. I want a man lying over me, always over me. His will, his pleasure, his desire, his life, his work, his sexuality the touchstone, my command, my pivot. I don't mind working, holding my ground intellectually, artistically; but as a woman, oh God, as a woman I want to be dominated. I don't mind being told to stand on my own two feet, not to cling, be all that I am capable of doing, but I am going to be pursued, fucked, possessed by the will of a male at his time, his bidding."

-Anais Nin

Women of zz's age were born in a time when women had very limited options. When women were able to land jobs they were often paid far less than men for the same work...no protection from the law. Cheap labor! The Moms of our generation were expected to be Happy Homemakers. That worked fine for many women, maybe even a majority. But one tragedy of discrimination was the many Moms with dynamic intellectual and creative skills who wanted to be out in the world, instead of bottled and capped, left at home living Thoreau's "lives of quiet desperation."

The tremendous social change of the 1960s gave women opportunities rarely before seen in all of human history. Not just jobs, but careers; not living off someone else, but bringing in their own money; dependence replaced by independence. Yet such freedom has its price.

Women either adopted, or tapped from within, qualities historically reserved for men: competitiveness, aggressiveness, confrontation, intimidation. Mental, physical and emotional toughness took center stage. That new suit fit many women, but in the long run others felt something important and vital to their femininity was missing.

Suddenly, after thirty or forty years of leading, there was a Primal urge, a calling from deep within...a need to surrender the mantle and pressure of leadership to a man, and be directed, cared for, and to obey.

To submit or not to submit, that is the question! The rightful application of such a question connects to an ancient human adage: does might make right, or right make might? Should the rule of force or the rule of law prevail? At this point in human history, humanity still aspires to rightful law ruling the world. Such are our hopes, while our reality is that misuse of power is common. So it goes in the world of domination/submission. If two people come to an agreement and each is happy with the ensuing roles and results, justice is in play.

If the leader uses power primarily for self- gratification, things are out of balance.

zz believed that using force and fear to dominate was a way of weakness. That's Abuse in any language.

He understood the submissive's quandary: finding a take charge personality deserving respect and trust. No easy bill to fill!

Although he had tried and tried, zz could not get his head all the way around the idea of submission. It was here zz's head froze. He could understand the idea of submission, but at that moment of submission he could not FEEL the insides of it. The desire to be free, so strong in his heart, obscured his view of the other side.

He had fought authority from birth...well, authority over him, that is. zz had always been a leader...growing up, on the job, in a relationship, and as a father. No problem being the authority figure!

Within the "submissive" group of women are many forms of submission. Some desire a man to take charge in all affairs of life, from what is worn to what friends are allowed to be seen. Others have a problem they cannot handle, like overeating, or extreme guilt when having sex. They want a disciplinarian to force them to desired behavior they cannot achieve themselves. A submissive may wish control to be a 24/7 arrangement, while others find something hiding or hindering their femininity is best remedied in the bedroom.

Bottom line? There is no one submissive personality...oh no! Variety is the spice of life! And there's no single road home.

It's commonly thought that the "submissive" is actually the leader in the relationship. Since the parameters and desires of the submissive are discussed and agreed to initially, it's really the dreams and desires of the submissive that drive the relationship. Some have felt submissive since childhood. They remember a constant need to serve, and going out of their way to make others happy. Others come to submission through many years of resistance, unable to reconcile their deep desires with their self-worth and dignity. Some submit easily and naturally, so anxious to please that a sharp look or a terse word will be like a slap in the face. Others find it just as natural to continually test, tease, dodge and dart their way through submission. Often such submissives enjoy and need physical punishment, perhaps even spanking. Such a woman was Lucy!

Lucy Dares DJ To Dance The D/s

"It's hard for an educated woman to turn her head off. That's part of the joy of being a submissive. None of the decisions are yours. When you can't refuse anything and can't even move, those voices in your head go silent. All you can do, and all you are permitted to do, is feel."

-Cherise Sinclair, "Dark Citadel"

There are a few reasons it's good to be the one and only DJ on the smallest radio station in the world. One great advantage is station revenue, and freedom from advertising. When it comes to ratings, there are none.

Thus, zz was able to play whatever music he wished, whenever he wished. Freedom to play the music he chose pleased him in a selfish way, but beyond that zz felt a call to duty.

zz knew that once upon a time there were all sorts of radio stations, where DJs wrote their own stuff, and created their own playlists. Nowadays DJs make announcements and promo anything under the sun. The playlists are arranged by market men who've studied stats to determine audiences, and preferences. No creativity and no variety...the radio is now primarily a graveyard of old songs, played in persistent memorial.

zz knew this demise ran directly back to the beloved Congress of the United States of America. Once again they had kissed

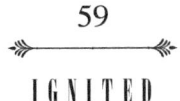

corporate America's ass and allowed ownership of several media outlets (radio, newspaper, TV), in a given market. Once upon a time there was a limit of two media outlets per geographic region, but that limit was removed. So now moguls own multiple outlets in multiple markets, and the same playlists are incorporated on a wide scale...even nationwide.

Thus many of the finest musicians have little or no access to the radio, and larger markets. Instead, they hit the road, putting it out there live each night. zz had recently jumped into the blues, so B.B. King, Eric Clapton, Jackie Greene, Keb Mo, Ruth Brown, Dr. John, Robert Cray, Ray Charles...the list rolls on. It was his priority to play the Good Old Days too: Beatles, all of Motown, Elton John, Paul Simon, Joni Mitchell, Jimi Hendrix, The Band, The Eagles, Bob Dylan, Van Halen...again, a long list goes on! His blossoming interest was African music, and what better way to leap in than with Ladysmith Black Mozambo, or the entire works of Johnny Clegg.

zz often said on the air, "Dr. Gravel Rasp and I do dedicate this station to those musicians...beautiful poetic troubadours. It's impossible to do all them honor...we barely scratch the surface. There they are, doing what they can, singing and shouting it out!"

zz's favorite part of the show was listener call-ins. These were very rare, as his schedule was odd, and his broadcasting range was the smallest in the world. Still, he did get listener calls, and spent many happy hours discussing This, That, and The Other. Yes, there were many interesting calls, but nobody lit him up like Lucy. Lucy had called in several times. They chitchatted music a bit, with other subjects as well. Politics, art, books, relationships...they shared many laughs and common convictions.

They spoke enough for him to gather bits and pieces of her past and present situations. Mother of one child, a daughter just finishing her senior year in college. She had been married ten years, and divorced ten. Lucy was fresh out of a six- year relationship with another woman. One day she awoke knowing that she wanted to have some male-order experiences. She ended her relationship, transferred job sites, found a place, and set out on her quest.

One day while chatting, out of the deep blue, Lucy asked him why there were no real men left in the world. Laughing aloud, he asked what she meant. She said that she could get a man to do what she wanted one way or another, and that she had almost given up finding a man that could tell her "No" and mean it. She was tired of wimps! She wanted a Real Man, one who took the lead and kept it.

Did zz know any such men? He again laughed, and said, "You're talking to him!"

It was her turn to have a hearty laugh! "I listen to your show a lot," she said, "and you are too too nice to be the man I hope to find!"

The challenge was on; they decided to meet. What other way to resolve this than a face-to-face showdown? They exchanged cell phone numbers and agreed to meet at the entrance of a large, busy park near her home, about an hour and a half drive for zz.

Lucy was Asian, with a Filipina mother and a Japanese father. She was about 5'4" tall, with shoulder length thick fine black hair. Her skin was soft with a golden glow and she had a naturally delicate, fresh scent.   She had an ample bosom. She was slow and resolute in her pace, and carried that weight like a Midwestern wife

IGNITED

crossing the kitchen, knowing nobody was eating until she cooked. Comfortably dressed in jeans and a white shirt with a black bra, she moved smilingly into zz for a hug.

zz wrapped his hugging arms around her. They fit politely for two seconds, when Lucy startled zz with a little extra-curricular movement of her chest and hips. "Never mind the stroll," she said, "follow me."

She walked ahead of him briskly, moving to the parking lot. She got to her car, a bright red Fiat convertible, and started the engine. What else to do? zz climbed in his ten-year-old Avalon, and followed her out of the parking lot. They arrived at her home moments later.

The moment they entered the doorway she turned for a kiss...a very aggressive, deep, swirling kiss emphasized with some hip gyrations. zz provided Lucy the first of her many surprises...he stepped away, walked into the living room and sat in an armchair. She let out a disappointed, peevish groan and paused momentarily with a little pout, then moved into the living room. As she passed in front of the armchair she got her next surprise:

"Stop!" he commanded.

She stopped walking, turned to look at him and said flippantly, "What? What do you want?"

"Turn and face me, stand straight and lace your hands behind your neck," he countered.

Their eyes met for a good minute...at first he thought he had misunderstood the whole situation! But she had felt something that scared and excited her simultaneously, like a traveler coming upon an oasis and fearing it to be a mirage. Suddenly embarrassed, she dropped her gaze to the floor, and laced her hands behind her neck.

Oh the smile zz smiled!!

"Pull your elbows back," zz ordered. "Thrust your breasts out." Feeling her pounding heart might break through her ribs, she did as ordered.

"You've already done some things that upset me," zz told her.

"We agreed to go for a walk. I like to take a walk when meeting; I learn so much watching the way a woman moves in the outdoors. Everything changes from the indoors, from make up to shoe style to conversation...words in the air differ from words within walls. You took all that away when you changed course."

He then stood up and moved behind her, and her nerves moved to the edge. With one hand he gripped her hair, while moving his right foot inside her right foot. He pushed her foot out, causing her to bend her knees and open her legs widely. zz continued his lecture, so pleased by Lucy's heavy breathing, and the scent of her wet sex.

"When we moved to the parking lot you didn't walk beside me, you walked in the lead." With that he gave her hair a sharp tug, pulling her head back. He put his mouth close to her ear, speaking in a low but intense tone.

"You lead me to the car, and took to the road without asking, or even telling me where we were going."

Giving her hair another tug, he slapped her ass hard, twice. When she dropped her hands to protect her rear, he ordered her to get them back where they belonged. She did, with a melting sigh.

"You moved to kiss me first!" he thundered. "What am I to do with you? You have no respect at all, do you? If you think you can shake a little, grind a little and lead me with words of promise, think again! I'm not even sure I want you yet!"

Her sighs were joined by moans...desire's harmony. With his next words she gasped sharply, nearly swooning...

"Ready for your spanking?"

zz moved across the room to the sofa and sat down. Lucy looked into his eyes...weighing and appraising. She shivered... his eyes meant business. They were firm, and intense...but not steely, or cold. There was even a hint of laughter, and the absolute certainty she would do as told.

She looked down at the ground, and hesitated...her second pause of the night. She was like Alice deciding if she should follow the rabbit into Wonderland, or Dorothy at the edge of the dark forest, pursuing Oz.

zz found so many things about women his age delightfully appealing. One was their toughness. They had experienced everything from giving birth to burying their most beloved. In the age of divorce they were often left with the children, and had managed somehow the single parenting life. Being very familiar with men and their ways, and having a variety of sexual experiences, older women were tough dates!

Battle tested and still standing strong, they had zz's admiration. Still, the lovely fragility of a woman removing her clothes for the first time in front of a lover! So vulnerable, soft, tentative, apprehensive, embarrassed, sooooo...enticing! He waited with patience and some amusement, watching the cacophony of thoughts and feelings run across her face. Finally she sighed deeply, and looked again into his eyes. Her eyes were soft, moist, demure.

"Come here," he said.

Lucy moved across the room awkwardly, nearly stumbling... then stood before him. "Take off your clothes."

Absolutely mortified, she started with her blouse. Her movements were slow, unsteady, reluctant...and then she was nude before him.

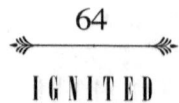

The feminine form! zz felt as though Van Gogh had sent him a newly finished canvas, just unwrapped. His senses were swirling. First he noticed her milky complexion, and the freckles scattered across her face, full-breasted chest, and strong firm legs the sun had tanned. Her sex was totally shaven, showing her already distended lips.

"Your skin glows," he told her, "it's healthy and vital; I want to kiss every inch of you. Your bare little pussy has me red hot; I love your round breasts and those thick, protruding brown nipples. And that lusciously curved rear end invites a spanking...and much more..."

She had a belly too large for her own satisfaction, despite her gym work, hiking and biking. zz was to learn that she had suffered two abdominal operations, one severing some muscles in her belly. Despite constant workouts, she could only do so much. Thus she was exceptionally sensitive and angry about that belly!

zz wished a potbelly was his only physical problem!

"Over my lap!" he commanded.

Lucy did as she was told...getting on all fours on the sofa and climbing over his lap. She did not know where her blood was pounding more! Her head was roaring like a river, currents pulling and pushing. Her sex was swollen, pounding, throbbing...on fire! Pressure rose from her chest out through her breasts, making her nipples feel as though they were being steadily pinched. Her thighs and belly were rubbing against his rough blue jeans, and her ass flamed with the feel of his eyes on her.

"You've been needing this for a long time, haven't you?" he asked.

"Y-yes," she whispered, barely able to speak.

He placed a forearm across her lower back, pushing her down.

The spanking began; he first gave her ten very hard and very fast swats, alternating right/left/right/left! She yelped and loudly, trying to wriggle away. "That's just ten," he said, and exploded ten more on her already reddened rear end.

She realized an anger she had never felt before, a fury with him for daring to do this, and with herself for allowing it! Again she tried to escape, wiggling and twisting against his hold...but to no avail. He was far too strong!

She was truly helpless! And again, a funny transition took place; realizing she really had no control, no power, the fury evaporated. She suddenly went limp, and felt a relaxed contentment. With a smile wide enough to split his mouth, zz stared at Lucy's lovely ass, heart shaped and heart colored, and began to massage it gently as he spoke to her. "There's nothing you can do to escape. No sweet or pleading tones will work...no bucking or fighting. You have no power...I have the power. All you can do is hope for the best; offer yourself to me! And we will find that boundary you are so anxious to chase!"

Whap! Whap! Whap! He began again, alternating speed, location, force. The spanking seemingly lasted forever...she twisted, writhed, bucked, cried, begged...nothing worked. He went on and on, telling her he would only stop when she proffered herself.

Soon she eagerly and wholeheartedly followed his commands. "Put your ass up in the air....offer it to me!" A new and shocking feeling overcame her...even as she was weeping, moaning, believing she couldn't stand the pain another second, she lifted herself in offering after each swat. There were no words left in her mind; time and space disappeared. There was only Him: his voice, his hands...the strength of his legs and swelling cock beneath the

IGNITED

blue jeans, and the relentless spanking!

The warmth from her ass spread through her belly, across her thighs and down behind her calves. It rose from her ass up her back along her spine, wrapping around her breasts and shoulders... her sex squirmed and ground against his jeans. Her low moaning sounds became a continual purrrrr...with strange sensations arising in and out of her, from every direction, she exploded in rocking orgasms...

He continued spanking through each orgasm, until the same instinct propelling him to action now brought him to a stop. As she shook with sobs, tears pouring down her cheeks, he stroked her shoulders, back, ass and legs, massaging her gently and thoroughly. She continued to cry and cry until he was worried he had gone too far, and done too much.

When she finally stopped, he found out his fears were groundless. She was weeping tears of joy, having at long last released something held in for so long. She laid still awhile more, and was nearly asleep when he moved, reaching for a pillow.

Placing the pillow on the ground between his legs, he ordered her off the sofa, to her knees. He undid his belt, unbuttoned and unzipped his jeans, and pulled them down over his knees and feet, tossing them in a nearby chair. He laughed aloud at her lust; she could not take her eyes from his sex.

"What a little slut you are," he teased. "Spanked like that and still hot for it!"

He leaned forward, grabbed her hair, and pulled her face near his sex.

"Beg to suck it," he said. "Make you mouth a hot little pussy... your lips pussy lips, your tongue a throbbing hot clit..." Oh how sincerely and completely she begged, tugging at his grip on her hair, trying to take in his sex...he roared like a lion as he came into her.

They spent the rest of the evening cuddling on the sofa; this time zz felt the embarrassment. Lucy found a thousand ways to tell him how wonderful she found him to be, and how long she had been writing for the "real thing."

Whenever zz heard such talk he counted it up to temporary insanity, and tried to smile as much as possible.

Lucy also let him in on much more of her lusty hopes and dreams. After a 6-year relationship with another woman, she had fantasies galore, and the daring and desire to try 'em out. And zz was the man to take her through the jungle!

Who said the surest way to make God laugh is making a future plan?

Lucy had two days to enjoy her good mood. She was called into her boss' office in the morning, and then she received a call from her sister in the afternoon.

Boss: Business is slow, you're laid off!

Sis: Mom fell and hurt her hip badly...can you help?

Within a week she was on the plane to Wisconsin. Ouch! No doubt zz was down and out discouraged by Lucy's twist of fate, and it's effect upon him...but he was also encouraged by two other online connections heating up. It reminded him of the story of the Sirens; two songs had him fascinated, and lost in a whirlpool of intrigue.

Isabelle Maella and Piper Murphy: dazzling Irish nymphs!

They had a common thread which prevented zz from seeing either one an much as he wanted, while seeing each of them exactly as much as they wanted: they were both married.

They had different approaches to being married and being on

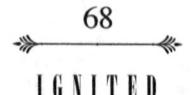

a dating site. Isabelle put out a profile hiding her pictures, sending them only if the man was a serious candidate for an affair. Piper listed her location as a major city hundreds of miles away. That way she did not show up in searches, yet was able to contact the men she was interested in, explaining her location and situation if sufficient momentum developed.

Seeking An Oasis

"Is this the land with the fountain of youth?"
-Ponce de Leon

Isabelle Maella decided one day she had had ENOUGH!
She either had to make a move and ease the growing, suffocating
pressure building within her, or possibly become unhinged.

As a child Belle had been bright and engaging from the get-
go. Her smile was brilliant, radiating genuine warmth, care and
affection. Her laugh was deep, heartfelt, and heard often. She
spoke and moved with ease and grace, admired and adored by
adults and popular among peers.

She had just turned 61 years old and looking in the mirror
after a shower. Her 5'6" Irish body had the prerequisite red hair
and freckles. She had been thick and curvy since childhood;
middle age hadn't changed her figure much. Her breasts were
small and still pert, and her bubble ass had an inviting bounce, ba-
boom ba-boom, when she moved.

Her face had the wrinkles common to a woman her age. When
tired, or ridden with anxiety, dark circles that had been etched
under her eyes during the decade of her daughter's seizures were
pronounced.

Looking in the mirror, staring into her own brown and hazel
eyes, she noticed a look of concern that had been in every picture
ever taken of her. She realized that from her earliest memories on
she had been more grounded and responsible than most adults.
She took on the role of caretaker very early in life, and had not

abandoned it since. The role suited her deep inner need to promote happiness within her and those around her; she could not stand disquiet or perturbation.

She had been born with a joy for life that somehow had grown over the years, despite the many times her life had come to the point, to paraphrase Eric Clapton, where she was crawlin' down a dead end street on her hands and knees.

Isabelle sailed through her childhood into her early twenties, continuing to charm, dazzle and achieve. Life certainly was not easy for her. Her parents were loving and very supportive, yet lacked financial resources. From the time she was in 6th grade Belle always had one or two part time jobs going. She spent little of her earnings. She saved saved saved!

Belle had also been gifted with a beautiful voice. Family and friends encouraged her to sing both for them and out in the world! So she did! Beginning at church, and also in school productions, she raised her voice in joy. She was invited to many types of gigs, but finally settled in with a blues band. She loved the piano, harmonica, and sax…this group had them all.

Her life was a wonderful whirlwind! School, work and singing kept moving and grooving. Only one thing missing…where was that man?

When meeting her husband she was taken with his bright energy, bursting with entrepreneurial possibilities. He was a big man, an ex-football player. She found his size and demeanor reassuring, inviting.

They went together a little over a year before he asked her to marry him. She hesitated. But her priest and parents assured her it was a blessed match, and they married just as she finished grad school and began her career as an assistant production manager for a prominent theater group. She was loving her job, and making good money.

In the beginning of their marriage her husband's investment ideas were solid, and they prospered. For the first time in her entire life, Isabelle felt she could relax where finances were concerned. She wasn't searching for riches, but having enough to pay the bills, have fun in life, and still save for a generous retirement gave her a new peace of mind.

The future had a golden glow.

However, the gold soon lost its glitter. Instead of having a marriage that heightened her carefree and blessed existence, Belle soon carried weight aplenty. Her husband's business actions fell far short of the dream. He engaged in a series of schemes that all failed. The last involved emptying their savings accounts without her knowledge.

As financial woes were mounting, there was a big change at work. The production manager resigned and moved to New York. Isabelle was offered the job and took it as much from necessity as desire. She was now working 60-70 hours a week, and making a six-figure income. It took her a decade to repay over half a million dollars of his debts.

While she worked so hard to pay off his errors in judgment, advancing her career as well, he went the opposite path. By the time she went online looking for a lover he had been unemployed a decade. He became passive-aggressive, and developed a habit of verbally demeaning her. Their passion had dwindled to a quickie every 3-4 months.

Isabelle's parenting experience nearly destroyed her.

Her eldest daughter, nearly finished with college, loved her and still spent as much time as possible with her. Daughter looked as much like her mother as possible, but had a very different

approach to the world. Whereas Isabelle's own happiness began with her keeping everyone happy and pleased, always seeking harmony, her daughter thought it much more important that people please her.

From the time she was two until nearly a teenager if she did not get her way she would kick, scream and cry for what seemed an eternity, stopping only when physically wasted, often throwing up in the process.

No adult was able to change her behavior, although many tried. The fits went on until puberty, when they were exchanged for a very aggressive attitude in getting what she wanted.

Her second daughter nearly caused her to crumble. Her list of maladies and the ensuing circumstances is long and fearfully awful. One example should suffice: it took ten years to find a combination of medicines that would stop the 8-10 serious seizures she was having every day.

There were many times, when one daughter lay wailing on the floor as her other daughter again convulsed, that she was terrified of spiraling out of control and never regaining a foothold…

When she began considering an affair, her family was in the best shape ever. Her daughter in college had excellent grades, a fine boyfriend, and loved spending time with her family, especially her Mama. Her second child was more stable and happy than ever in her life, although she still had little control over her bowels, and often needed cleaning. Also, she was a couple of inches and 25 pounds heavier than her mother, and when frustrated would attack physically.

Although lacking as a spouse, her husband was a wonderful father. Both his children loved him. He also was there daily for their youngest, and physically capable of dealing with her. Since the need for tranquility and harmony were threads of Isabelle's heart, the idea of decimating this relative calm for her family froze her.

Isabelle came to the conclusion that divorce would be the ruination of too much that was hard earned and a long time coming. Not only with her family dynamics, but with money as well. Her husband had no income. She was paying her daughter's way through college. The financial necessities attending her second daughter's condition, including trying to build a trust for when Belle could no longer care for her, were substantial. She had mortgage payments and if divorced there would be alimony payments too! It had taken years to regain financial footing after her husband's debts were honored; she could not endure the idea of another fall, and again starting over.

Despite carrying the weight of being the sole supporter of her family, a passionless marriage, and quite a burden of motherhood, Belle may have remained staid into old age, except for the growing realization that the side of her that had always sustained and enlivened her, her creative and sensuous nature, was dying. That's when she knew she had to begin anew, and seek revival.

She went to see some live music. She and her oldest daughter went to the ballet often. With her busy schedule she couldn't do much more, but it was a start.

As soon as time permitted, she vowed to again delve into her singing!

And although she tried as hard as any good Catholic girl with a guilty conscience could possibly try, she could not allow her erotic passion to wither into dust. The pure need for a man was difficult enough to try and manage, but then these wild fantasies and images arrived, moved in, and would not leave!

She created a false identity, withheld her picture from the public eye, and began searching for a lover…

When zz first contacted her, Belle was being pursued by many, including a surgeon who wanted to put her on airplanes and fly her to fine dining and hotels in the places of her choice. With his introductory note, zz included poetry and copies of drawings he had done.

Although he was a decade older than she wanted, and short and wiry where she liked big and brawny, once they began communicating they were lost in a whirling dervish. They met soon after writing and speaking, and took a long leisurely walk, filled with fascination, flirting and laughter.

Isabelle shocked herself and went against all her prior training and actions; she agreed their next meeting would be a hotel. That began their love affair, meeting every week or two for hours of lovemaking.

zz loved to occasionally tease her about being so "easy," but told her not to worry…he liked sluts! She would stare at him with her Irishfeisty perking inside, eyes ablaze, searching for a comeback and finding none but laughter…

Honeywater

*"I have a lifetime appointment and I intend to serve it.
I expect to die at 110, shot by a jealous husband."*

-Thurgood Marshall, the first
African-American member of the U.S. Supreme Court

As always, zz arrived first. He moved into the lobby and arranged for the room, carrying in two bags. One had candles, a corkscrew, music, his three cherry, a book on dream interpretation by Betty Bethards, and…at her request…his high school graduation picture.

The other was a grocery bag. As it was winter and the air was biting, soup was the main dish. Today it was a spicy chicken lentil. There was a long loaf of crusty French bread, and a bottle of Chardonnay. Fruit: blueberries, raspberries, blackberries. Always chocolate: one dark chocolate bar with bits of orange rind, and a milk chocolate bar with caramel swirls. A bouquet of flowers rose above the top of the bag. No doubt about it, zz had it bad for Isabelle.

zz always brought more than enough so she could take leftovers for lunch the following day. The chocolate bars were large and would last her through the week.

Entering the room zz set the bags down and got busy. First, he arranged the food on a wooden coffee table; they preferred eating while sitting on the sofa, next to each other. Along with the food he lit two scented candles, one watermelon and the other tropical.

He then got his laptop, which included music and a small

book he made for her each meeting. As Christmas was near, zz brought a Christmas music compilation he had worked on for years, with many selections. The book was a sonnet that contained about 20 verses over 20 pages, and on each page an image matching the verse. The sonnets absolutely melted Isabelle, or, as he sometimes called her, Belle.

With the candles burning zz moved furniture about to suit his purposes. Between each meeting they flirted heavily, via text, emails and phone calls. There were always some scenes worth trying in person.

There was no part of sex Isabelle did not relish. Years of frustration needed amending! She craved penetration from every position and angle. When they first met she had not been with anyone matching zz's intensity and endurance, but by their third meeting she was meeting each thrust with vigor. She also loved getting her hands and mouth on zz's sex; at times he thought she might even enjoy it as much as chocolate.

But her magnificent obsession was being on the receiving end of oral sex. During the week zz had teased her with two fantasies that would be reality very soon. First, he took a blanket and covered the kitchen table. He had often told her she was his best dessert…today she would be. He would place her up on the table, pull up a chair, have her put her legs over his shoulders…dessert is served!

He took a blanket from the bed, double folded it and put it over the table. He also got a pillow from the bed and put it on the table against the wall so she could recline comfortably.

Finished with the table, he crossed the room and grabbed an armchair, moving it directly in front of, and facing, a floor length mirror. Belle would be seated in that chair, with zz on his knees, between her legs. As he was busy, she could look into the mirror and see him worshipping that saucy sex!

With the table and chair now set, he moved to the bed. He put a pillow in the middle of the bed. When he had her on her hands and knees he would put the pillow under her to further raise and open her.

Just about done! He lit the candles, and then went to the windows and pulled the curtains tight against the light. With all that done, he started the music, smoked some three cherry, and thought of Isabelle and her incredible orgasms, the like of which he had never seen before.

With some of her orgasms his lovely Belle gushed honeywater. When she gushed, not only did her cum flow, but also a stream of water that poured and poured.

The combination was intoxicating!

A small percentage of women release water with some of their orgasms. The amount of water, and the way it is released, varies. Some women release a flood, as did Isabelle, while others a stream, or tributary. Some women pour, some spurt like a geyser... Isabelle gushed. It was as if an underwater lake escaped, broke through the surface, creating a new pond. A pond in which zz loved skinnydippin'!

He waited another 15 minutes and the knock came... His heart upped its tempo. He jumped to the door. As Isabelle eased in the door zz eased into her, wrapping her up in his arms and alternating soft, lipbrush kisses with long hot swirls...

After a few minutes of kissing zz helped Isabelle remove her coat, and hung it on the rack by the door. As they resumed kissing zz combined a massage with slowly removing her clothes. She dressed with a purpose: sometimes long zippers, another time a single hook, and an occasional tease with a long row of small buttons. This time she was winter-layered. After he removed all layers except her panties, they moved to the table.

Smiling, she put a foot on the chair, climbed on the table, and lay back against the pillow.

Ordinarily zz would take his sweet time, have Belle on the bed, and kiss every inch of her body. Today he could not wait for a taste he had come to crave: her sweet sex. He sat on the chair, reached out and unhooked her bra, rolled down her panties, and put them on the table. He put her legs over his shoulders. His hands moved to her breasts, cupping them and squeezing gently while he kissed her thighs, belly, and triangle above her sex.

Instantaneously she was sopping wet, moaning, moving, pushing her hips toward him, and spreading her legs as widely as possible, opening to him completely. How he savored his view, and her scent filling the room.

Isabelle kept her sex neatly trimmed. She did not like waxing because of itching…although she would have shaved if zz so preferred. She had the tiniest, cutest sex zz had ever seen. And like a person, it had many moods and faces.

When he started her sexlips were already red and swollen tight together, almost as in a pouting frown, upset they weren't getting enough attention. He began to licking, sucking, and even gently chewing those throbbing inflamed lips as her moaning and groaning turned to whimpering and pleading.

He forced his tongue inside her sex, near her ass, away from her clit. For 20-30 strokes he pushed his tongue in and out, while his fingers began kneading her areolas. Her entire body shifted, pushing toward him while throwing her arms back, her legs splayed, inviting…even her mouth wide open, with its chorus of

79

sexsounds. Every part of her stretched wide open in offering. zz was moaning himself!

As he moved up her sex toward her clit, she begged "Pleasepleaseplease!" He had to stop a moment and smile…and as he did she groaned in disappointment. Once upon a time she had scoffed at the notion that she would ever beg him, or anybody else, for anything! "Are you sincerely begging me?" he asked calmly.

"God…yesyesyes! PLEASE!"

With that he moved to her clit. He reached for her panties and shocked her by pushing part of them into her sex. He started flicking the tip of his tongue up and down, back and forth across that clit for a very short time before Isabelle began to yell out a come. With hips bucking, thighs tightening around his head, belly writhing and sex lifting to the ceiling her shrieks could be heard echoing off the halls and out into the corridor, down to the lobby. zz often wondered who might be outside enjoying the concert.

As she came, initially a thick cum descended. Warm, flowing slowly, and tasting like her own brand of honey…zz sucked and licked it into his mouth while continuing to flick and suck on her clit. Then the first water trickled from around the sides of her sex, rolling easily around all sides of his mouth. He drank! But then the gush! Suddenly a flood of water, pond emerging, and zz's entire face and beard were submerged as the water poured down, through her panties and the covers, splashing down onto the floor, making a puddle!

The water reminded zz of spring water! It was fresh and clear as could be, with a clean sweet taste. Mix with her honey cum… honeywater! zz loved to drink as much as he could catch. This time on a whim he did not swallow, but took a mouth full of her Cum and moved up to her, kissing her and releasing her cum into her mouth.

"Taste it," he said in a low growl..."see how sweet and wonderful you taste!"

Belle was in a state of constant amazement with her lover... he often shocked her. She drank and smiled widely, surprisingly pleased with her own taste...

He helped her down as they moved to the bed, her legs a little shaky. She was very embarrassed by the flooded floor, but zz assured her it was awesomely sexy!

He put her on her back, kissed her, smiled into her eyes and slid back down to her sex. Isabelle was unlike any woman he had known. With every woman he had known, once they had an orgasm their clit was far too sensitive for any more stimulation. Following a huge orgasm if zz continued touching that now very sensitive clit, bad things followed. He had been yelled at, squeezed nearly to death by clenched thighs, and even shoved off the bed by clits that had had just about enough, thank you!

Isabelle was quite the opposite. Her first enormous cum was just a beginning...her soaking slick sex shouted for more! Again he started on her lips, this time grabbing them lightly in his teeth, and pulling them...pull, nibble, lick and kiss...until soon he had her clit in his mouth, this time sucking gently while swishing juices over her hot button. On and on he went, up and down her sexlips, penetrating with his tongue, and again and again returning to that burning clit. zz didn't even pause a bit between orgasms; he continued relentlessly, and she loved it! She came three more times, but only once more with the fervent flow of honeywater.

As usual, their lovemaking lasted hours, until they fell asleep, her spooning into him, curled up and feeling secure, protected... and sexually spent!

Volcanic Eruptions

"I spent half my money on gambling, alcohol and wild women. The other half I wasted."

-W.C. Fields

When he returned home the next morning, zz was beat, and crashed into bed for a long winter's nap. As he slept, he dreamed…and what a dream it was! He saw women he had dated in a cavalcade of cunnilingual cum convulsions…

He awoke with a tremendous smile on his face and quickly was up out of bed; he was a man on a glorious mission! Memory lane had come calling in delightful fashion!

Moving to the kitchen he brewed a cup of tea, adding the usual dash of milk with three heaping spoonfuls of sugar. He had a small study in the front of the house, with large French windows that looked out on three streets converging in a T shape, with his study at the top center of the T. Carrying the cup to his study, he sat at his desk, sipped, and let his memory wander from woman to woman, comparing orgasms.

Feminine orgasms were like earthquakes: no two ever exactly identical. They varied in force, source, depth, movement, location, duration, and accompanying sounds. Add in the million possible moods of a woman and it's obvious there are too many variables for any system of comprehension, much less predictions. But what fun is the exploring process!!!

Orgasms with small tremors could arise from an infinite number of sources. A neck massage, reading erotica, shower water running over the clit, a hot memory, nipples rubbing the inside of the bra or squeezing thighs together…any of these could set one off. It could be riding a bike, feeling the sex move against the seat one day, then again on that same bike the next day because of the way the sun warms the thighs.

Smaller orgasms also came often as aftershocks to the main tremor, alone or one after the other in a sort of sequence…

It's tempting to say these small orgasms are also resigned to a particular area, like the sex, but it just isn't so. One time the heat may rise in the clit followed by a little explosion, another time that same heat sends tremors down the inside of the thighs, through the calves and right into the soles of the feet. Orgasms stem from the breasts, staying there…or ripple from the breasts into the belly, neck and back. On and on, ad infinitum…lucky women!

Large, full orgasms are another breed altogether. Whatever the lady's specialty might be (groans, howls, shrieks, moans, screams) the volume will be turned up to maximum. Walls and ceiling will reverberate; if the neighbors hear, they never look at her the same way again.

As with minor tremors location, movement and duration can vary extensively. Sometimes the eruption is sudden, violent and local like a volcano shooting lava high up in the air. Her sex spasms, the heat and tremor staying in her rocking vulva. The next time that same swift orgasm may move in different directions, the tremor simultaneously moving from her sex down her legs, through her ass and up her back and spine, and across her belly up through her breasts and into her neck and face.

Major orgasms usually, but certainly not always, originated from the sex. Lucy had cum long and hard, more than once, while being spanked. Naneeka had body-shaking orgasms from having her breasts stroked and sucked. Isabelle had surprised herself by having a long, shaking orgasm while zz tongue fucked her ass.

IGNITED

The most powerful, tsunami causing orgasms have emotional release involved. Women making love after a long absence, maybe due to child rearing, a divorce, or being a widow, have incredible orgasms that first time out! Of course a whole lot of the steam and fire is pure reaction to having gone without for so long. But what gives that cum tsunami strength are feelings. The sexual release is also releasing the past, and the hold it has on her. Sounds a little funny, but that orgasm is her future arriving in style!

His memory moved through women he had known, comparing styles of orgasms. Three of his lovers had orgasmic styles that he would not have believed had he not experienced them himself. Once during a spanking Lucy had cum for 45 straight minutes. 45 minutes! Observing it wore zz out; when she finally stopped Lucy cried for 15 minutes as zz held her. She then slept for hours.

Naneeka had warned him from the start that when she had a top of the charts orgasm, she would pass out for up to five minutes. Pass out! Knocked out by a cum! Even though he had been forewarned, the first time she had blacked out zz fought the urge to call 911 until she awoke.

Finally Belle, and her precious honeywater. Mmmmmmmm...

While thinking of the many varieties of female orgasms, and the lovers he had experienced, zz's attention moved to memories of being on the receiving end of oral sex.

That gave him an idea! He logged onto his computer and started searching through erotica left him by his lovers. He searched for, and found where each one left him an oral sex scene they had written for him after the fact...a sort of memento.

Unable to stand his erection jammed against his jeans any longer, zz unbuckled his belt, unbuttoned his fly, ran down his zipper, tugged his sex out and idly stroked it with his left hand while scrolling with his right hand, reading their steamy descriptions.

From Lucy:

Friday evening is my favorite night of the week. This is my "goodbye work week" time and I usually let nothing interfere with my special, private Friday night unwind. I start the evening with glass of red wine, sounds of jazz and lots of candles. Tonight I am expecting a visitor.

When my lover arrives, I greet him at the door, already hot and wet. Anticipation is everything. After we sit down on the sofa, I taste his lips, tongue, neck, and dart my tongue in his ears, making him moan.

I slowly undress him, kissing, and licking, sucking every inch of his beautiful body. He is writhing and moaning softly with his baritone voice. I stop for a moment, and lead him to my big white leather chair, positioning his legs in a wide "V."

I take his not quite fully swollen cock in my hands, gently stroking up and down. I take my time exploring, tasting, savoring his enormous sex. I finally take him into my mouth, first the quivering head, then slowly work my way down to the base, circling around and around back to the knob. I love hearing his loud moans of pleasure, and his increasing thrusting, as each minute becomes more and more intense. I want to touch, taste, relish every inch of his cock.

Time disappears as I use my hands and mouth, moving from the top of his cock back to the bottom, over and over…I cannot get enough! Finally, as I deep throat him like a piston churning, he roars and pushes me from him, telling me to get on the bed…

IGNITED

I quickly walk to the bedroom and climb on the bed, face down as he likes, beside the 4 long silk scarves I found on sale last week…

zz remembered it had been difficult to get from the leather chair to the bedroom. He was wobbly and shaking, heated and engorged near bursting. His cock bobbed in the air as he walked, with an occasional spasm making it twitch and lift.

He could not have held off taking her if it were not for the silk scarves. By the time he had one around each of her wrists and ankles, and secured them to the bedpost, he had regained control. Finished tying her down, he loved the contrast of her skin tones with the dark red scarves. He spanked her until her ass was the color of the scarves, then took her in a hurried, intense burst.

Remembering Lucy and her deepthroating him upped the speed of zz's left hand. He slouched in the chair to get a better angle for masturbating as he brought up Naneeka's scene.

Naneeka:

We have been at it for a while on that beach in Alameda, tucked in the dunes on a Friday morning. Getting to know each other. We hug, kiss…lovely, rich erotic language flows back and forth, turning your member hard and firm. Through your jeans, I feel it growing. The breeze is gentle through the Golden Gate and the sand beneath us groans. Beach walkers vanish into the mist.

I turn. You answer. I drop to my knees, reach out to unbuckle, pull your jeans to your knees as you squirm to release your confined cock.

I lean forward and slowly, with my tongue, draw circles on the crown. Your cock stiffens further, touched by my tongue, reaching out to embrace its wet, warm juices. We are speaking a special language at that moment.

Then, without pause, I take your fullness deep into my mouth. All the way in. I close my lips around the base, my nose buried in your rough hair. My lips are blood-full and pulsing. I breathe in, picking up the faint scent of sandalwood…I love a man who bathes well!

Then, very slowly at first, I suck sweetly, pulling back and forth. The rhythms of ancient drums fill the air. Back and forth. In and out. Juices dripping from my fevered lips. Your member growing hot, full…ready to burst.

Pulsing with each drum beat. Back and forth. In and out. And then, in a moment, a geyser of joy spilled forth and filling my mouth with bliss as your body ripples with energy released fully.

zz was now in a dither. His left hand had become a blur while reading and remembering that day on the beach with Naneeka. He groaned while stopping himself from spurting, removing his hand and staring down at the veins pulsing on the side of his sex. "Not yet, pal!" he told his aching cock. "One to go!"

He very gingerly caressed his knob, emitted a long low growl, while moving to another pounding description…

Isabelle:

There it was in front of my face, a smooth sweet cock for the sucking. I had not realized in my younger years of sexual experience the joy of having a man's cock in my mouth. All such was foreign and strange back then. Now as a quite experienced woman of 61 I craved the warm sensations of moving my hands and mouth up and down my lover's hard shaft.

On his knees over my face, his penis was so inviting. I flicked my tongue quickly under the hood and firmly ran both hands up

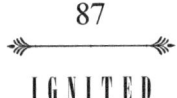

to his testicles and back to the velvet head. Soon the precum was whetting my appetite for more. The taste was sweetly salty as his hips involuntarily gyrated.

Excitement building, he spun around to suck my clit and I now had him in my mouth from another direction. I controlled his thrusting with my hand, taking my fill of him. His excitement continued to build while wave after wave of orgasms rolled through me.

I maneuvered him over to his back and went down on my hands and knees between his legs. I pushed my warm breasts over his cock and balls, keeping them in my cleavage while holding him tightly. He moaned louder and began to slide his cock up and down between my breasts.

Able to wait no longer I lowered my mouth to his member and resumed sucking, pumping, kissing and licking him. My head hit his belly again and again as I climaxed with a sudden explosion.

His cock and balls red hot, his cock throbbing, his thrusting a blur. He bellers as he spurts his tasty fluid into my mouth. I wait until his spasms stop, then run my tongue lightly over the head, moving down to kiss his penis, belly and thighs.
Heaven on earth.

zz certainly agreed with heaven on earth; he could hold back no longer. His ass rocked his desk chair back and forth as he spurted his cum for what seemed hours...

Suddenly exhausted, he reclined in his chair for a morning nap. When he awoke he looked at the clock through groggy eyes and gasped! He was a half hour late calling another very dissatisfied wife, and very satisfied lover: Piper Murphy!

Red

"At the end of three days, moving Southward, you come upon Anastasia, a city with concentric canals watering it and kites flying over it. I should tell you of the women I have seen bathing in the pool of a garden and who sometimes-- it is said--invite the stranger to disrobe with them and chase them in the water."

-Italo Calvino, "*Invisible Cities*"

Pics sometimes capture the eye. This lady has long flowing red hair, and the freckles and smooth milky white complexion to prove it's natural. zz had a theory that hair is the brain turned inside out; look at Einstein! Red has waves of curling, swirling locks...a fiery waterfall! Her eyes dance in their sparkle; she moves mountains with her energy, quick tongue, sensuality, imagination and a keen intellect! Quite a wit in the world...

Her other pics don't hurt. In one she has a saloon style costume pushing her breasts up high, and in another a man is laying face up on the ground, her spike heels resting on his chest. Her firm breasts, strong legs and smooth complexion had zz hurting; over time he received many lusty and artful pictures from Red, all the way from her magnificent pool house to her flaming red and recently self-paddled ass...

She is on the dating site despite being married! Murphy's husband adores her, and she him. They spend nearly all their time away from work together. Sharing a crossword, strolling through downtown, out to a company event, or walking their two dogs.

Profile name? Taken from a favorite aunt: Piper Murphy.

Why would a woman living the dream have an alias, and a profile on a dating site? Guess? Bedroom. She is a steaming, fantasy-filled, sexually bubbling cauldron, and he...about once a month, maybe less, a five-minute ride in the missionary style. In every other aspect of their shared existence, he is dominant... running the finances, questioning her on her activities, rebuking her for a poorly cooked meal, or mussed cushion on the sofa.

It's hard on a woman if her man gapes at other women, or has an affair...but nothing hurts a woman's femininity worse than a man cold to her touch.

A few months before contacting Piper Murphy, fantasies fresh and new to zz began to intrude. That's right, intrude. Scenes and situations were coming up that shocked and embarrassed him privately, right to the core. He'd hoped they were a curiosity, not to last, yet time increased their force.

zz began to search for profiles where the woman liked taking charge. How he had no idea, but a 73-year-old dominant woman from Harlem messaged him, admiring his profile. After exchanging a few notes, he wrote her of his desire to explore being led by a woman. Then things got very interesting! zz had fun, and learned he was dominant through and through...but the sort of dominant who finds it relaxing once in awhile to let his Lady use her creativity and imagination to tease and please him.. To this day he is friends with Her Majesty from Harlem...

When zz saw Piper Murphy standing with her boots on a man's chest, whip in hand...those livewire eyes! He copypasted one of his notes to the Harlem Queen, and sent it to Piper... accidentally sending the salutation from the previous letter! Turns out Ms. Piper had desires of complete submission, and zz had called her by a wrong name, just for starters. How could it be that soon he'd have her write him while sitting nude in a chair, legs spread, open in offering?

Thankfully, after reading his profile, she was intrigued. So when he wrote back with an apology, telling her of his error, and the fact he was dominant by nature, she accepted the truth. They exchanged letters, each letter examining the "me Tarzan, you Jane" philosophy.

Piper Murphy has fierce pride, nobility and strength of character...in the workaday world she submits to no one. But erotically she tried to end run it, deny it, reason against and snub it...but the urge to have a man take over and lead the way sexually was consuming her. In that sense, her marriage was the fire under the boiling teapot, converting water to steamy exploration.

After a couple of notes, zz gave her the first erotic order: whenever she wrote to him, or read his letters, she was to keep her legs wide open...preferably without panties. She had powerful responses to that command. From a very early age females are taught to keep themselves concealed, not revealed. Cross your legs, pull down your skirt, place a hand between the knees when you sit down in a dress...but whatever you do, do not allow a man to get even a glimpse of those private parts!

Piper Murphy meekly agreed to follow that first command. She was submissive, and yearned for a strong man to take charge. Yet her experience in the world was quite the opposite. She doesn't distrust men because of fear or intimidation; she distrusts men because men are so easily lead and controlled.

Piper Murphy knew full well how to use her feminine wiles to move men as she would. She leads conversation adroitly, with a nod of ascension, or a simple change of subject. She always includes a little line of flirtation, while leaning over a little with her low cut dress, enjoying his wandering eyes, amused by how easily he loses control. She asks questions to which she already knows the answer, for two reasons: checking on the man's knowledge while allowing him to supply the answer and be the authority.

She is an expert at having a man believe he has thought up her ideas, leading him while laughing with a flutter at his jokes. She is as hard to catch as a butterfly: stretching her wings, darting, dodging, rising and falling just out of reach....

Red had all but given up believing there could be a man able to understand her, and use that understanding to control her. Right from the start, she had to test him.

He would ask her if she had opened herself when reading his note, but she would "forget." After three such lapses he asked her what should happen when she failed to do as ordered? She agreed some sort of punishment would be necessary...that's when she e-mailed zz the pic of her red and bruised ass, from an episode with her one and only experience with a dom. She communicated with the dom online only, never speaking with him on the phone or meeting in person. It stung her hard when he vanished one day, without ever supplying an explanation.

She had taken a wooden paddle to herself at his command, and done so viciously. Expecting more of the same, she was puzzled yet relieved when all I asked her to get was a long leather shoelace...its use to be revealed later.

It wasn't long before we had shifted from online to the phone. Once there Miss Piper Murphy melted...moaning, pleading and whimpering...she had more sweet sounds than a symphony. Those sounds made zz crazy wild with desire...

At this point she started keeping a diary for zz...

Piper's Diary

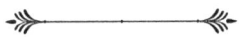

*"It isn't that you are not incredible at it, nor that
I hate to let you go...but I do not want to hold you
back...and limit you...so now I am torn..."*

-Piper

My diary should probably start back to the aftermath of our
wonderful (for me!) playing the other night. I know you assumed
that I would want to immediately go satisfy myself to relieve the
intense pressure of excitement I felt...but...surprisingly (for me!)
I did not. Instead, I fell into the most deep sleep I have had for
months...so awakening a mere 45 minutes before I was due at work
was both a pleasant surprise and a problem... And then, in that
short time frame...I read your e-mail and you gave me specific
instructions. Even with my time line, I was able to manage the first
two...to be in the positions...briefly...and I did blush...they really
are very...well...rude?...positions...and they made me wet (yes, my
legs are wide apart now...and I am not wearing panties, just tight
black trousers).

Last night I read all of our communications. I'm afraid
I stayed up rather late doing that...and having looooong
conversations with you in my head... But...that meant I went back
to rereading our first Contact...the message that you sent that you
said defined you...and now...now... I am feeling like I am being
very selfish by wanting you to be my "Sir." You made it clear that
you now wanted to explore a different direction...and...and I...

well...I'm dragging you back down to a place you wanted to move out of.

It isn't that you are not incredible at it, nor that I hate to let you go...but I do not want to hold you back...and limit you...so now I am torn...Please tell me what would please you. You...not me... what you need for me to grow and be satisfied. Even if it means I lose you...well, I will be sad, but that is selfish...and I would be more pleased if you were soaring personally.
Your Piper

After that, their exchanges became heated, wild...zz had her doing more and more outrageous tasks, and she more than rose to the challenge. At the time who would have known they were rolling too fast, shattering too many barriers, like a jet plane tearing the sky...

zz sent back a note with Piper's next assignment:

Stand in front of a mirror, nude. Imagine I sit there, not the mirror. The purpose of the mirror is to have you see you as I see you.

Open your legs and pull your sex lips apart, showing the inside of your sex. See how red, swollen? Pull back the lips and reveal your clit. Stare at it for a minute, imagining me sitting there before you, stroking my thickening cock, enjoying your hunger.

Now, walk about your living room nude, for a minute or two. Exaggerate the natural swing of your hips, imagining me walking behind you, demanding sluttiness. I have my whip in hand, to be sure.

Now, walk about your living room nude, for a minute or two.

Exaggerate the natural swing of your hips, imagining me walking behind you, demanding sluttiness. I have my whip in hand, to be sure.

Dear Sir:

*Standing in front of a mirror, imagining you there instead...
well, there are a couple of things I do not like about my body and
I should confess them now. My stomach has swollen and my waist
is larger...(as in...12 inches larger) than it was for most of my adult
life. I am changing those, but right now they dominate what I focus
on when I look into any mirror and I would not want to disgust you.*

*On the other hand...my breasts...well, I really like them.
And my legs...and...well, you asked me to look at...and display...
something else...something I've never looked at really, and
certainly not in this position. You know what? They were cute,
too. My labia and my little hard clit. I don't have any basis for
comparison, so it was just my viewpoint, not any media messages,
but seriously...kinda sweet.*

*The leather lace? I think we need to discuss this more so that
I am using what you wish...I just grabbed a boot lace from my
container of shoelaces...and it is probably too long...too rough...
too...well...if you wouldn't mind letting me know what you had in
mind exactly...*

*Pinching any part of my nipples...aureoles...breasts...
is...hard...I have never played with my lips like that...I don't
know which part of it was more exciting...or maybe it was the
combination of everything, including that you were starting to send
me e-mails wondering why I hadn't done as you asked.. I had very
good reasons, but I was anxious all the same...and felt bad I hadn't
been able to do so immediately.*
Piper

*Finally growing a little sleepy. But I know what I am going to
dream about.*

Piper Murphy! By now she was in zz's thoughts and dreams continually. So sensuous, bright, coquettish, and with a great flair or the dramatic. She should have been an actress, commanding attention onstage.

Originally zz believed Piper grew up wealthy and pampered. Nothing like that in her background. Her father worked hard fishing off the coast of Maine. He was a gentle soul, yet all man. She loved being near him. His eyes were alive, engaging, and calm. His skin was rough and ruddy from working on the ocean, and his hands were tough, efficient, and gentle. He had endless patience, and a tremendous love for his daughter. She was and remains Daddy's little girl.

Her relationship with her mom really wasn't. Mom was cold and critical in handling her daughter. Communications came in two forms: orders, or instructions on how to improve yet another found fault. Incredible some parents out there! Miss Piper Murphy is brilliant and was always a superior student. She speaks and writes with elegance and warmth, and she is conscientious far beyond the call of duty. What Mom was wanting is anyone's guess, but most parents in the entire history of parenting would have cherished such a child.

After her marriage and move to the West Coast, Luc, her husband, hit it big with the inception of the .com explosion. They had not come from wealth, but had wealth now, and adjusted nicely to the advantages. For instance, Luc had originally gone on a special diet, and Piper cooked accordingly. But when his diet became gluten free, and then additional stipulations were added, she gave up! Wanting help she hired a chef to cook the specially ordained grub. There are spas, personal trainers, dieticians, massages....

Wealth or none, Piper Murphy had Dignity. Her husband, Luc, also from a modest background, found that out big time. Luc grew up in Southern California, in the San Fernando Valley, and met Piper while attending U.C.L.A.

Like zz, Luc had a paper route when he was a kid. He delivered his papers about two miles from his house, but it seemed a million miles away. He pedaled out of a nice middle class neighborhood into vast, rolling estates. At that time he vowed not only to move into the neighborhood, but also to have the home of his dreams.

When he came to 1625 Oak Harbor Drive, he got off his bike so he could walk the paper to the front door of the huge Victorian, surrounded by incredible gardens. This knight had found his castle.

After college and marriage, Luc put his Big Brain to work in the emerging internet explosion, making them rich. Although he had the technical expertise, Piper had the business acumen. A true partnership was the foundation of their success. With a small fortune tucked away, Luc could not believe his good luck when the house he had long coveted hit the market. He rushed Piper to see it, and she too loved it! They made an offer that night, without haggling the price at all.

Over the next week Piper noticed a disturbing trend in Luc's thinking. Apparently his vision of the future had his wife doing the bulk of keeping the castle, while he went off to work. That became a serious area of contention between the two of them. Piper demanded he verbally commit to splitting the duties of the estate. Luc absolutely refused to say he would do half the work necessary to keep such a place, when business was already taking all his time. Piper saw that overseeing the house alone would keep her at home full time.

97

Many folks had offered on the house, but they were selected. He was in 7th heaven, oblivious to her increasing resentment. The papers were due on December 20th, but Luc was away on a business trip. Piper had to attend the meeting alone.

When he returned on the 21st, Luc learned the papers had ended up in the fireplace, and the house belonged to another couple.

"That's when he learned just how strong I am," she said.

From Piper's diary...
I was just at the grocery store, and, since it was a Saturday, there were several husband/wife couples shopping. I'm assuming they were married; I wasn't looking for wedding rings. What was truly astounding was that every single one of them...I could tell, even not hearing the full conversation...the woman was belittling or mocking or implying the husband was an ignorant ass in some way, and the man would respond with what was obvious (at least to me) barely controlled fury, even though they never raised their voice...I could tell they were beyond frustrated angry.

I tried to keep away from these people; you never know when someone is going to snap and I could be collateral damage. I'm assuming that you aren't jealous of my husband, merely the thought of me catting around with other OKC guys...I promise I won't talk a lot about him, but...This afternoon, as we walked back to the car after lunch, I said, "I love you."

Luc replied, "As well you should." It made me laugh.

I just got home from doing errands, and said to Luc, who was reading, "I'm sorry darling, they did not have any ripe bananas. Would you like an orange? Or some mixed fruit?"

"Mixed fruit."

So, I took the plastic container of berries and a fork over to the chair where he was sitting, handed him the container (I was expecting him to object that I had not put them in a glass bowl) and started to give him the fork, when he just opened his mouth wide, so that I could feed him a strawberry.

I thought, "oh my god. I've been married to a dom all these years, just not a sexual one."

P i p e r t o y

"It is essential that we realize once and for all that man is much more of a sexual creature than a moral creature. Sex is inherent; morals are grafted on."

-Emma Goldman

Our passion now accelerated and we had to meet. She told zz more than once that her unfulfilled desires were undermining her love for her husband. She was irritable, critical, snapping at him. People can get to a point where there is no turning back. A problem lingers and it can no longer be tolerated. Then frustration and loneliness become routine along with desperation for something special. Something long repressed has pounded at the door until it finally opens. A wanderer in the desert, seeking an Oasis.

The pressure must be relieved, like a hot boiler's steam let out with a valve; otherwise, her whole world is in danger of blowing up! An affair can be that Oasis, and relieve that pressure. In Piper Murphy's situation, she believed that once she began her affair, the immense resentment she held toward her husband would evaporate. Life is chock full of amazing contradictions!

Luckily for the two of them her husband was called to Washington D.C. for a week. They rented a very nice suite of three rooms for that week, pretending it was their own. What a week it was! It's possible later down the road to look at such moments with wistfulness, missing what one doesn't have. Not for zz...such an adventure became part of his heart's memory.

When he's low down in mood or action, the moments of sweet memories past rejuvenate!

Her husband left Sunday night. zz checked in Sunday morning, to arrange certain things according to needs. Monday morning they both went off to work as usual.

From Piper's diary:

I approached the front door after work with more trepidation than usual. I now had a new reason to dread Mondays, other than they were the most jam-packed days at work. Sir had declared Monday to be "punishment day" and that meant my night was going to be difficult, to say the least.

While digging my key out of my bag, I reviewed the weekend. I thought I had been good. The problem was that I always thought that, yet Sir always found areas where I had been less than adequate. How hard could it be to keep one man happy? I groused as I let myself in.

The box was there, the key in the lock. I knew what that meant. He expected me to remove all my clothes. Again?! This was getting...well...honestly...I would have expected the novelty of a naked Piper in front of him to have worn off long before this. Surely I could be permitted to wear something while at home?

Sighing, I kicked off my heels, unbuttoned my blouse and removed it, followed by my skirt. It was true that diet and near constant "exercise" had improved my figure, but I still had all the body anxiety issues that any 59-year- old woman in a culture of 17-year-old airbrushed supermodels and cosmetically enhanced playmate bunny porn stars would have.

I unhooked my bra and slipped out of my panties and my stockings with reluctance. Unlocking the box, I found the expected note of instructions. There was also a collar. This was a new one;

one I had never seen before. It was of thick black leather, with four rings evenly spaced around it. I felt my stomach tighten. The worst part of Punishment Monday was never knowing what fresh hell Sir's inventive mind would dream up. But this did not look good, not at all. On the other hand...there was no leash. And it wasn't the dog collar. Being his puppy was not one of my favorite ways to end a workday, to say the least. I reluctantly buckled the collar on. Then I placed all of my clothes in the box, along with my handbag, removing the one item I knew that he would request, and locked the box.

Unfolding the note, I read "Living Room." I hesitated, still trying to think of anything I could have done wrong. I was trying so very hard to be perfect and yet still failing in his eyes. I bit my lip. Stalling was probably a bad idea, too. No matter how quietly I managed to slip into the house, somehow he always knew exactly when I was home. That was a mystery I still hadn't figured out.

Taking a deep breath, I picked up the key and the other thing and walked into the living room.

Sir was in an armchair, reading the newspaper, a cup of tea on the table beside him. He did not rise, as a gentleman would, but waited instead for me to cross to him and kiss him. Smiling, he said, "Welcome home, Piper," and he held out his hand. I placed the key from the box in it, and he slipped it into his pocket. There would be no more clothes for me until it was time to dress for work in the morning.

Then, he raised his eyebrows as he held out his hand again. Nervously, I surrendered my iPhone, hoping there was nothing on it of which he would disapprove. He said nothing; merely laying it down beside his tea.

He made a movement of his head, indicating something behind me. Turning, I saw a new piece of...well, furniture wasn't quite the *right word. It was a solid-looking wooden bench. And, jutting out of it was a...a...well, a phallus. It was obscene.*

I quickly looked back and objected, "Sir! You can't mean for me to..."

"Quiet." His command cut off my protest and let me know I wasn't going to be allowed to speak again. "Hurry up!"

A second jerk of his chin directed me to the bench. That knot in my stomach had just grown to monstrous size. Clearly, he wanted me to mount myself on the...the...thing on the bench while he watched. I didn't really have any alternative, so I clambered onto the bench. It was high enough so that the balls of my feet barely touched the floor, and I had to use my hands to lift myself up high enough to get above the cock.

"Look at me," Sir instructed, and so I looked into his eyes, watching as he watched my every move in return.

I carefully positioned myself above the fake cock, then started to slowly lower myself onto it, my hands gripping the sides of the narrow bench for leverage. The thing was as thick as Sir himself, but I was relieved to note not as long, otherwise this would have been utterly impossible.

I whimpered as it sank deeply into me, and Sir smiled. When my bottom finally touched the bench, he got up and walked over to me. Grabbing my right hand from the bench, he tied it to the ring on the right side of my collar and then did the same with my left hand, before returning to his armchair. He sat down, took a sip of his tea and continued to watch me.

With my arms above my waist, my center of gravity had shifted, and I was struggling to maintain my balance. Teetering on my toes, any dignity already lost, I realized there was no way to lift myself off – I was trapped on it until Sir decided otherwise.

"Position, Piper," he snapped.

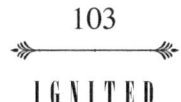

I straightened my spine and pushed my shoulders back, thrusting my breasts out, my nipples pointed towards the sky. My legs were already spread by the bench, but I did my best to open them wider.

Sir watched and smiled, so clearly I was doing something right. Perhaps he was in a good mood and this would be a light night, I thought hopefully.

What I hadn't counted on was how wet I was becoming. I had been aroused just walking into the living room; by now my body was conditioned to respond erotically whenever Sir was present. But the phallus was..... was... opening me. And my struggle for balance was making it stimulate me in a very filthy way. A demeaning way. Still... wiggling around on it felt really, really good. I had been so aroused all day...oh, heck, who was I kidding? I was now constantly aroused and no matter how often I came, the arousal came right back, driving me mad with desire most of the time.

"Piper. Hold STILL."

The muscles of my sex were convulsively squeezing and releasing the phallus, desperate for the feel of a real cock... well, Sir's cock, actually.

All the while I was struggling to hold my balance...my position...and to not wiggle. I had a sudden flash of how much more I could enjoy this if I were wearing heels, since then I could push myself up and down on the cock, pleasuring myself... if the heels were very high, that is. I was turning beet red at the idea of wearing nothing but high heels and a leather collar, impaled on a phallus in the living room for someone else's pleasure erotic. Yet I was now so wet I was trickling moisture onto the wood of the bench. What had happened to me?

I watched Sir's face carefully, as he made his review, trying to determine what he was thinking. Exactly how much trouble was I in? As Sir's hand reached down and undid the zipper on his jeans, freeing his cock. I licked my lips and bounced a little bit, hoping he would be too distracted to notice.

Sir began to stroke himself and I half groaned, half whimpered. If he made himself cum... without using me in any way to suck him or, even better, to put his cock where the damnable phallus was continuing to trap and torment me... then there would be no relief for me tonight. I wished this had been one of the nights when he was so eager for me that he just took me right away. I tried to hold back another moan and worried that I might be drooling. I could smell the musk of him from here, and it was intoxicating.

Sir finally looked up at me, and studied me carefully. My face reddened with embarrassment and arousal, my little nipples hard with desire, my hair falling around my shoulders wildly tangled as I kept trying to jerk my hands free of the collar... my thighs tense with the effort of keeping my legs spread wide...my swollen sex clearly visible over the phallus, with the wetness seeping down. God... he must be able to smell me, too! I could imagine how I looked and it wasn't ladylike in any way at all.

"Do you have any idea what submission means, Piper? I am not sure you do. I think that's something we should work on tonight, don't you?"

I gulped. No, Sir wasn't in a good mood. And no, it wasn't going to be an easy night. But, on the plus side...he had not cum yet... so there was a chance...

I ducked my head down low, submissively. To hide my smile...

Work, and then "home" to such a wondrous woman! It would take an entire novel to recount that week. They had discussions ranging far and wide: religion, childhoods, developments in

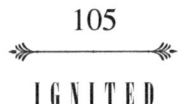

technology...on and on! Within each discussion they shared lively and spirited teasing, wordplay...

She was absolutely intoxicating; she was adventurous and imaginative in all she did...charming, witty...and oh so wild. Together they pushed limits that had only been dreams, filaments of fantasy. Her erotic desires and imagination knew no boundaries, and pushed zz past what he had anticipated. They each had intense personalities, and those intensities combined nearly consumed them; each morning it grew more and more difficult to pull their wasted bodies from bed. Yet each night passion would rise to new wildness, ending in near frenzied cumming...

The next to last night...

In many ways, she was never more in touch with her femininity than when she was begging him. Not begging to please or cajole him…no, it came from the heart. Once upon a time she had believed she would never ever beg, and she again sighed…this Man! The first time she was nearly mad, out of her mind….lost in a world beyond thought and words, yet raging with a passion she had never felt before. He had tied her face down, nude, with a large pillow under her, elevating, spreading her hips. Her head was near the foot of the bed…which faced large closet doors covered with mirrors. "Eventually," zz said, "this will be one of the positions you assume on command. That will be after some training…very necessary for one like you."

For a long time he had sat behind her, staring at her "offerings." Try as she might, a hot flush began to spread through, over her…and she was surprised to feel so embarrassed! Every once in awhile he would lean forward, and lightly blow air over her sex, ass…gently running fingernails down her back, over her thighs, calves.

She began to moan, wriggle…he slapped each asscheek---solid whacks. "Be still," he ordered.

zz then climbed off the bed, walked to the foot, and stood facing her.

He held his enormous erection in his hand, lightly stroking it, just out of her lips' reach. He grabbed her hair with one hand, and lifted her eyes to his. He then thrust his huge erection into her mouth, up to his balls…she gagged as she felt his balls resting on her chin. Just as suddenly he pulled out, still holding her head up by her hair, and reached with his free hand down to her ass…and gave each cheek another slap. He then pulled her eyes down to see his cock wet from her mouth. How she wanted that sex in her, penetrating, plunging…again she moaned, twisted.

He walked back and climbed on the bed, between her legs… and put the tip of his cock against her sex. She tried moving back to take it, be taken…but again her ass was slapped. "How red and swollen those pussy lips are," he said. "See your juices on your thighs…so hot, soaking, throbbing." He took each of her asscheeks in hand, spreading her as widely as he could.

Quickly…very quickly…he tongued her sex, asshole…she moaned loudly, squirming and arching to meet his tongue…

Swiftly zz sat up, thrust his muscled thighs between her legs, splitting her more open. He grabbed her hair, pulling her head up.

"You have no self-control at all, do you?"

Taking her panties from the chair, he got behind her, covered two fingers with the panties, and entered her. He enjoyed her moaning, and thrusting her hips. As soon as she caught the rhythm, he abruptly stopped. "These panties are soaked!" he said, pretending anger.

zz then stuffed her mouth with the panties, grinning. "That should keep you quiet…"

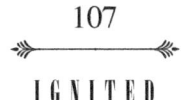

IGNITED

Again he was on the bed, between her legs. "Let's play," he said.

Reaching forward he first grabbed one of her pussy lips with his hand, and then the other with his other hand. He began slowly kneading, pinching, stroking them with his fingers, top to bottom, over and over again, never touching that precious little clit…no matter how many times he used this technique, it never failed to bring passion to astounding heights, for both of them.

Finally, taking cock in hand, zz moved the thick, swollen knob slowly up and down her opening….how eagerly she wiggles her hips, trying to slide onto him. He slaps each cheek 2-3 times; "Be still!"

He moves up tighter to her, placing his knees and thighs inside hers, and uses the leverage to open her even wider, pinning her in place at the same time. Still holding his cock with one hand, he places the off hand between her shoulder blades, holding her down. Then he pushes the top half of the knob--- only the top half---into the very middle of her lips. He feels how hot, swollen,
throbbing and very tight they are….

He puts his mouth near her ear, and whispers, "In a moment, if you beg…truly beg… if I hear your heart, and your little pussy, beg with all their might, I'll put it in. Remember," he said, "I know the difference between begging for show, and sincerity… Now beg for it!"

Oh how she pleased him, wanting penetration so much as to surrender all   pride and plead so earnestly! As he pushed his way past those swollen lips, the thick knob and shaft splitting her, she moaned over and over, an animal in heat…messages from a world beyond words, ideas…

The next morning the joy of being together was bittersweet,

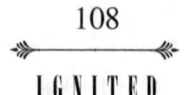

knowing it was the last day they would come "home" to each other...

They exchanged a long, silent hug and kiss before she left for work...

After she left for work he moved all of passion's toys back to his car; he held each item as though it were fragile, filled with sizzling memories, hot to the touch.

On the way home zz had a smile wide enough to split his face. Isabelle and Piper were extremely successful and busy professionals. It was all they could do to get away every week or two for a few hours of steamed heat. With just one of them, he would have likely steeped in frustration. But with two? He laughed aloud; two would do...

That day he played a nothing but love songs driven by a dancing beat.

zz Gets ZZ'd

"Brevity is the soul of lingerie"

-Dorothy Parker

As usual, just when we think Life moves to our beat and rhythm, Life sends us a wake up call; who's in charge? This came in the form of a phone call from a friend from college days, Yvette. She was one of two people who had loaned him a substantial sum of money when he was on the way to the bottom.

As soon as he landed his DJ job he began making monthly payments, but it would be years before he could repay her.

Her call was surprising, but she had an even greater surprise in store for him. She told him the week before she was with an old friend, Esmeralda. The two of them got very drunk, and magnificently horny! Yvette brought out some spicy stories zz had written for her. The two had quite a time reading, drinking, and lusting!

She said Esmeralda called the next day and asked about him, while confiding she had experienced some incredibly explosive masturbation, inspired by the stories. She wanted to meet him. She also had a moneymaking proposition for some significant cash!

Esmeralda was Chairwoman of the Reno Arts and Entertainment Council. The City of Reno was hosting a musical festival for a week in about 3 months. They needed a combination M.C./DJ, and the job paid exceptionally well. Well enough for zz to repay all he owed Yvette, and more! For hosting a music festival!

Zowie!

Yvette said there was just one "condition."

zz was Amazingly Attentive.

Knowing Yvette was a horse trader nonpareil, zz was getting the "Yeah, right...too good to be true" feeling. zz asked what the "condition" might be?

Yvette said he had to surrender to her for one night.

"Surrender?" he said.

"You'll have to trust me on that one" she replied, flashing her most mischievous smile!

She told him to be there the following Saturday about six o' clock in the evening to help with a 64th birthday surprise for Esmeralda.

"And that would be?" he asked.

"It won't cost you more than a birthday suit," she said with a smile of pure mischief. Leaning forward, whispering in his ear, she laid out the terms. By the time she was done, zz was blushing a furious crimson, while nodding in embarrassed agreement.

A week later, he was at Esmeralda's door...birthday suited!!!

Birthday Suited

"Ours is not to reason why,
Ours is but to do or die."

-"Charge of the Light Brigade"
-Alfred Lord Tennyson

When Yvette, her best friend, said she had the best birthday present ever, and keep the night free for her, Esmeralda did so without reservation or hesitation. They had been best of friends for over 20 years, and she had never heard such hyperbole from Yvette before. "I'll be over about eight to pick you up," her friend said, "wear something supersexy!"

Esmeralda decided to wear her black Hawaiian floral print dress with a neckline almost exposing her wide, soft pink areolas, and tiny pink nipples. She laughed aloud, thinking of how many men would be captivated.

A bit before 8:00 there was a knock at the door, which surprised her; Yvette had her own key to the house. Esmeralda went to the peephole, flicked on the porch light and gasped to near choking! Falling back from the door she gasped again and reddened deeply, through and through. Gathering what composure she could, she opened the door and saw that her shocking pal had vanished, leaving only "the gift" behind.

Suddenly realizing a neighbor could easily pass by and see, she grabbed the silken cord attached to the collar and pulled him in the door, shaking...

Although he could not see her, she felt tremendous

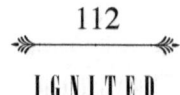

embarrassment...and momentarily dropped her eyes, lost in a fierce blush.

Except for the collar around his neck and the blindfold, he was nude! His hands were lashed together in front of him with one end of a black silk cord; the other end of the cord was attached to a ring in the collar around his neck. A short red silk cord was tied around the base of his enormous manhood, and written on that swollen sex, in erasable marker: Happy Birthday!

It was all too much! She nearly swooned. Then laughter overcame her...Yvette!!

The nervousness soon vanished, replaced by a fire...her sex suddenly burning, itching...needing. It had been a long time. She took the red cord, and smiled when he jumped from her touch.

Tugging slightly on his "leash," she led him across the room, walking backwards to enjoy the view.

His sex...mmmmm...erect, bouncing as he walked...wide, thick, long...a tremendous knob that looked like a real red plum had been attached. He was circumcised, with thick veins, swollen and throbbing, even more pronounced from the cord tied around the base, nestled in red pubic hair...

Yvette had delivered an award winning cock!

"Stand still, "she said to him, again smiling as he followed her command, awkwardly...maybe with a little resistance? Slowing down for a moment she stared at his face, and searched for what he felt. To her delight, she sensed most his utter embarrassment. She wondered how he was convinced to do this!

Her eyes dropped slowly down his ruddy, freckled body. Neck, shoulders, chest...all looked like he had been a football player, or picked crops, or worked in a mine. Broad, defined...and that same look ran from his shoulders through his biceps, forearms and big hands. There was no hair on his shoulders or back, but across his chest and on his arms the hair was full, and soft...moved from red to gray and white. He had a little potbelly but very little extra weight. Her sex was on fire... She reached out and took his sex, grabbing the middle of the shaft. He shivered, uttering a frustrated groan as a tremor shook his body...

So sensitive! She soon had him singing songs of moans and growls...when his hips began to thrust back and forth as if he was making love to the air, she tugged at the silk cord and started leading him again, enjoying his unsteady walk and low, disappointed ooooooo...

They moved down the hallway to her bedroom, and across the bedroom to an armchair. She stopped him just before the chair, moved around behind him, and pressed against him, reaching around with both hands for his distended cock. Again he convulsed with her touch...she stroked him for a few moments, then moved her hands to his ass, cupping and squeezing...and little scratches, which drew soft hisses from him. She took her hands from his ass, put one on each of his shoulders and pressured him to his knees.

What a sight! While admiring the view she lifted her dress and removed her fire red panties, tossing them on the bed. She walked around the chair, and sat. Opening her legs she put one over each of his shoulders, while grabbing his hair and pulling his face to her burning sex. She exploded in moments, wailing out a cum that coursed from the Source though her entire body--an electrical tidal wave.

Crudely she shoved him back, nearly knocking him over, as she fell in a heap in the chair. After recovering, she helped him to his feet and to the bed. She had him climb up on the bed and lay him face down, spreadeagled. She untied the loop from his collar and tied his hands to an opening in the middle of the headboard.

Climbing on the bed, she placed herself behind him, and moved onto his back, her legs straddling him just above his ass. Slowly she began gliding her slippery sex up and down his spine; how he did groan! The feel of his strong back and her sex split by his spine was sooo sweet! Next, she lay down full length on top of him, her breasts mashed against his shoulders, and her legs between his, pushing him open; she wanted him out of control, gone down the road, burning with a hurting desire.

Grabbing his hair with one hand and pushing herself up with the other hand, she told him to get up on his knees, but leave his head and shoulders on the mattress.

She pulled him backward until the cord tying his hands was almost taut, reached for a pillow, and placed it under his belly, further elevating his hips.

She placed her knees inside his and opened him as widely as he could stand, her breasts rubbing his back. She moved her hips in and out of his, as though she were doing him from behind... She was surprised and so pleased as he fell into the rhythm... Not wanting him tooooo happy yet, she abruptly stopped, moved upright on her knees, and leaned back for a moment, her hand moving across her clit as she stared at him, ass up in the air, long scrotum dangling, pulsing blue veins on his balls as he thrust back and forth in vain...all the while an aaaaaaarrrrghhhhh from deep in his belly as his head moved side to side.

It was all too much! Erupting again, she was, for a moment, woozy...

As she settled, she moved against him again, her sex feeling the heat of those balls. Reaching under him she cupped and stroked his balls with one hand, while circling her hand around his sex, midway up that fatted shaft. The red silk cord, tight like a cock ring, was deliciously denying him that release for which he was

115

now incredibly and pathetically desperate. His dignity was gone; he would do anything to have his orgasm!

She began to pump his cock slowly, up near the knob, back down to the silk, up again...all the while lightly rubbing, cupping, and circling his balls. He was now thrusting back and forth so hard she had to hold on--it was no longer necessary to pump his cock; she held her hand in place and he used it like a sex...

Then she stopped all, and got off the bed...the poor man was humping the pillow, saying "please please   please," making sounds within sounds...sharp gasps and pleas into sobbing, begging near weeping...

Esmeralda pulled the pillow out from under him, pushed him up on his knees, untied the black cord from his collar, and slid under him, wrapping her legs around him, while swallowing his sex with hers.

They gasped and flew in mutual mad delight as he fucked her with a primitive savage fury, his cock a steaming piston...

One of her hands reached out, and yanked the slipknot holding the red ribbon from the base of his cock, releasing his sex...roaring out a beastly cum, lion in the jungle, he thrust his full and spurting sex into her screaming orgasm...

Esmeralda's eyes opened she received another shock on this amazing 64th birthday; Yvette was in the hallway, leaning against the wall, her hand inside her jeans...smiling a mile wide smile. With swiveling hips and screaming out a powerful cummmm, she slid slowly down the wall to the floor...

After being untied and given his freedom, zz found his clothes had been delivered to the bathroom. He dressed to the tune of two women singing a duet in French, punctuated with raucous laughter.

He scurried down the hall and sorta slunk himself home. Once there, he crashed onto his bed, and into some powerful dreams.

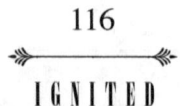

He awoke knowing he had discovered a paradox of his own that evening: every moment of the previous night had mortified AND excited him.

Help!

Forked Road

"When you come to a fork in the road, take it."

-Yogi Berra

From the content of the story one might assume all zz did for years was datedatedate...not so! He spent 10-12 hours a day on the radio business, bringing along some regular hours, lively call in exchanges, and a small, devoted following. zz believed his "followers" to be a dementedly off kilter and possibly dangerous bunch.

Since the station had some promos and ads, he also received many tickets to concerts. Thus he was often out the door to live music. Shake and bake! He worked hard rebuilding some vital relationships. For the first time in his life he was on good terms with his Mom, brother, kids and grandkids. Once again he orbited in a known and unified universe.

Camping had again become a priority. Nothing too bold; he liked flushing toilets :) Still, from the beach on up to the mountain streams he pitched his tent and rekindled a love of the outdoors.

Inside of him the joy of freedom lit him up like a sky full of fireworks...corny but true!

And the women…Zowie!

Naneeka was currently and monogamously involved. Her new joy was radiant...and that joy was contagious! Her smile spread to his face when he thought of her good fortune. And zz was absolutely sure that if things happened to fall apart for her, he would be there to help in every way…

Lucy was off on her mission, but e-mails and phone calls kept them in touch. She says it's only a matter of time until she returns.

Isabelle and Piper were lighting off his fireworks on a regular basis now; both lovely ladies had settled into harmonic rhythms in his life.

zz would have died of shame if anyone knew how often he thought of Yvette and Esmeralda. He had been ready to leave it at that when he got an e-mail from Esmeralda a couple of weeks after her birthday, wondering if he might like to drop by when she returned from a lengthly trip to France...

Sitting in his home at the desk in his studio, spinning out Spirited Tunes with vim and vigor, zz's head swirled in amazement and wonder at the possibilities open to him, here on the eve of his 60th birthday.

zz was chock-full of marvel and wonder. Not so long ago he had been isolated, alone on a desolate island, casting messages in bottles out into the vast sea. Against all odds a new life had come in with the tide.

He was going to catch this unexpected, delightful new wave, and ride it all the way to shore.

IGNITED

IGNITED

ABOUT THE AUTHOR

When I was in high school my English teacher, Lawrence McLaughlin, told our class that we would have a decent time on the planet if we managed to avoid two things: jail and mental asylums.

So far so good.